PRAISE FOR [illegible] YNN RUBIN

"With echoes of Francesca [illegible] Hinton, *Burro Hills* feels like a fever dream: dark, dangerous, but full of beauty so raw it hurts. Jack and Connor have all of my heart, and so does Julia Lynn Rubin."

—Rebecca Christiansen, author of *Maybe in Paris*

"With raw intensity and complex characters, Rubin opens a world of emotions that will resonate with readers."

—Jessica Kapp, author of *Body Parts*

"Rubin's writing is vivid and exciting. I was hooked on Jack from beginning to end. Set in a flashy California town, an interesting romance blossoms in this important coming-of-age story."

—Lisa M. Cronkhite, author of *Fix Me*

"*Burro Hills* is pure grit and heart. It has everything my reckless teenage self would have wanted (needed) from a book. Jack is the best friend I had in high school, and *Burro Hills* is the town I desperately wanted to leave. This struck deep in my guts and will resonate for quite some time. Brave, bold, wild and honest."

—Bonnie Pipkin, author of *Aftercare Instructions*

"Julia Lynn Rubin crafts Jack's journey of self discovery with pitch-perfect dialogue and page-turning tension. Rife with dysfunctional families and complicated romance, *Burro Hills* is a vivid portrait of one teen's search for acceptance."

—Gillian French, author of *The Lies They Tell*

"Julia Lynn Rubin draws beautifully complicated characters and an utterly convincing world. This book is gritty, unflinching and full of heart."

—Meredith Miller, author of *Little Wrecks*

BURRO HILLS

JULIA LYNN RUBIN

DIVERSIONBOOKS

Diversion Books
A Division of Diversion Publishing Corp.
443 Park Avenue South, Suite 1008
New York, New York 10016
www.DiversionBooks.com

For more information, email info@diversionbooks.com

First Diversion Books edition March 2018.
Paperback ISBN: 978-1-63576-194-8
eBook ISBN: 978-1-63576-193-1

LSIDB/1802

Carve your name into my arm
Instead of stressed, I lie here charmed
—Placebo, "Every You Every Me"

1

Show-off. That was the first thing I thought about Connor Orellana. *Fucking show-off.*

But it paid off for him.

Connor came to Burro Hills the spring semester of my junior year, transferring in from a school about an hour south of here in a little town called Creek Way. It was the year Mom lost her job as a movie theater ticket taker, the latest in a long succession of odd jobs, and the year that my father said he'd finally stop drinking and succeeded for more than a month. It was a spring of intense heat, fires burning a hole through the forested mountains, trailing plumes of heavy smoke into the white-hot sky. Looking back now on that time, the smoke seems like a signal, a warning or an omen of some kind. I knew Connor would change the game for me; I had no idea just how much.

It was late April. I was squinting through my sunglasses from my usual spot on the steps out front after school, waiting for my boys to finish fucking around at their lockers so we could ride home together, like we usually did. That's when I spotted him up close, and something changed in the air as I watched him. Something sparked. There was this bold new kid with an expensive-looking skateboard, doing ollies and slick freestyles in front of a gathering crowd. And it kind of pissed me off. It was hot as hell that day, but this kid had just turned up the heat a notch higher than it rightfully should've been.

Connor was an instant hit with some of the cutest girls at school since he'd arrived back in January. But now that the weather was growing warmer, the wildfires increasing in intensity in the hills and the mountains, he was outside more often, showing off for them. Those same girls got moony-eyed and giggly when he'd swerve around a group of them on his board, turning around to wink at them and hear them squeal. In the halls, freshmen girls talked about how they loved the way he spiked the front of his jet-black hair, and how lean his body looked when he took off his shirt in the sun.

He was a show-off for sure, and rumor had it he was a *criminal.*

I heard it first earlier that year from Jess between snaps of her bubblegum. He'd been to juvie apparently, kicked out of St. Francis High School in Creek Way for punching the principal and breaking his nose. Smoked a lot of weed, slept with a lot of nearly unattainable girls—or so that was his alleged resume. I brushed it off at first. It was Jess. She ate up Bigfoot specials and ghost hunter shows. As much as I loved her, she wasn't always a credible source and neither were the dumbass kids at our school.

But the more I saw of him that semester, the more those urban legends seemed like they might have some truth behind them. Only a few months had gone by, and already it seemed like his name was on everyone's lips, or at least the people that ran in my circle. *Connor Orellana,* his imagined deeds ingrained into Burro Hills High School lore. The rest of them either whispered about him in the hallway or blew him off as another loser, a junkie or a deadbeat's son like the rest of us. I was hopelessly intrigued.

He was in my math class for a few weeks until he was transferred into the Honors section, and this one time, I watched him slide a note to one of the hottest girls in school, some bleached-blonde bimbo named Maggie Turner. She'd wrinkled her nose and opened it carefully, like it was full of anthrax, then rolled her eyes and passed it to her girlfriends and some of the football team assholes in the back of the room. They'd thought it was hysterical, laughing and making comments like fifth graders, saying "fucking faggot" and that kind of thing. Someone had rolled the note in a little ball and tossed it at Connor's head. I watched to see what he'd do, if he'd get pissed or something, but he just sat there grinning like an idiot, like he was the only one really in on the joke. Then he caught me looking at him and held my gaze for a second too long. I remember the warm rush I got, like I was in on the joke now too. And as the football assholes eventually simmered down and went back to talking about sports and all their bullshit, Connor pulled a pair of Ray Bans from his bag and slipped them on, slouching in his chair. Goodnight, assholes.

He didn't mind eating alone for the first few months or so—seemed to view it as some rite of passage—or walking to class alone through the sea of blank faces, earbuds lodged in his ears, snapping his fingers to an invisible beat. He spotted me in the hallway once and grinned that ridiculous grin of his. I'd nodded and tried to keep a straight face, but after he'd passed I couldn't stop smiling to myself. I didn't fully understand at the time what was happening, or why my eyes were always glued to him, but it was as if we were connected by some invisible but inevitable force.

And then that hot day in April came, when the spark happened, when that intangible shift in the universe occurred as he did tricks just a few feet away from where I was sitting on the steps. I'd been thinking about it for a while now, but it felt like the right time. I convinced the boys to let him come with us on one of our freeway rides after school. They readily agreed. They'd watched him do his board tricks and light up fat blunts during lunch and before school for weeks on end, smoking right under security's noses. Naturally he'd hang out with us, they said.

Naturally, my ass. It was my idea.

"What did you *really* do?" Max asked him the first time he came out for a ride. The air that day was thick with exhaust fumes that got stuck inside your throat. Connor sped ahead of him to do a few wheelies. Max pedaled hard to catch up, his sweat-soaked *Looney Tunes* shirt sticking to his back, his dark hair matted against his neck. I trailed behind, just close enough to hear them.

"What do you mean?" asked Connor. He kept his focus ahead, on something across the horizon. Max panted like a bulldog and pedaled faster, nearly running over a spare tire on the side of the road.

"At your old school," Toby broke in, a familiar sneer on his face. "St. Francis. Don't play dumb, man. You know what people say."

Connor squinted up at the burning blue sky, rolling

his neck around. I watched his jaw clench up, the square muscle pulsing. "People say a lot of things, don't they?"

I cleared my throat to let the guys know I had this. "Just a couple things about getting kicked out and all that." I paused to see how he'd react. "Breaking the principal's nose, you know..."

Connor's face remained unreadable. "If I had touched the principal's nose, would I even be walking around right now?"

Max was gasping for breath at that point, trying with all his might to ride as fast as Connor. "So, is any of it true?"

I opened my mouth to say something else, but Connor did a quick circle around us before pedaling fast ahead, trailing dirt and dust behind him as he rode into the edge of the sun.

2

Max was sweating bullets and the car hadn't even pulled up yet.

Toby and I stood watch, hands in our pockets, trying to assume an air of nonchalance. A James Dean casual, cool, *don't-fuck-with-me* stance. Usually we did these deals alone, under the cover of dusk, but Toby had insisted Max come at least once and stop being such a pussy about the whole ordeal.

"Do we have to do it here?" Max whined. He wiped his face on his Star Trek t-shirt and pulled his beanie down over his face. Toby yanked it off his head.

"Cut it out," Toby growled. "I told you if you wanted to come, you had to be cool about it."

I gave Max a pat on the back. "It'll be fine, man. Just relax."

Max cracked his knuckles like he always did when he was nervous and took a deep breath. He tried his best to turn his face to cold, uncaring stone. The Shop N' Save parking lot was just off the freeway, the roar of engines and occasional honks of angry drivers echoing across the wide expanse of concrete. It was cooler now that the sun was beginning to set, the sky a blend of buttery yellow and smashed orange.

I checked my watch. Toby glanced over his shoulder, then stiffened suddenly, nodding in the direction of the store.

Jess was here. *Fuck, fuck, fuck.* She was trailed by Anna and Lizzie, her two faithful, pretty-girl companions, and something about her was different. The bounce in her step was still there, the girlish way she popped her bubblegum and twirled her hair—yes, that was it! Her once raven-colored hair was now a bright, platinum blonde.

It was just hair, just hair, I kept telling myself, *girls always change their hair,* but for some reason it made me feel itchy all over, like when someone pronounces your last name wrong and you really want to correct them. She looked like a piece of candy, a bright, sunny popsicle. She looked like all the other bimbo girls at our school.

She looked like her fucking *sister.*

"Hey boys!" Anna called out. She wrapped an arm around Max, and he blushed the color of his scarlet beanie that Toby was now pulling apart by the threads.

"What you up to?" Lizzie asked. Every time she spoke, it made me think of a wind-up toy, dizzy and spinning and squeaking.

Jess smiled at me, the secret Jess-and-Jack smile, the smile she usually gave me when we were alone in her room or my room playing Xbox or smoking pot or staring up at the ceiling, talking about our darkest fears and secrets and dreams of escape from this shitty little town. She couldn't be here. The car would pull up any minute, they'd see the girls, the girls would see them, and the whole world would explode.

"Nothing, just business," Toby said, leaning into Lizzie. She rolled her eyes and shot a knowing look at the girls. What the hell was he doing flirting now? Didn't he see how precarious this situation was?

"Five minutes, Tobe," I said, but it came out more like a cough. The girls frowned at me in confusion. Toby just shrugged. My eyes kept falling back on the freeway, watching for that one, burnt orange SUV to pull up any second now. For now, I could only see a blur of beige and black and white speeding down the road. Why did everyone pick the same damn color for their car?

"So, who wants pizza?" Max asked. "I'm really hungry. Matter of fact, I could definitely go for a slice right now. I mean, it's really important to eat three solid meals a day, nutritionally speaking, although pizza isn't—"

Toby kicked Max in the shin and Lizzie giggled.

"You guys should go," I said to the girls.

Anna scowled at me. Lizzie crossed her arms over her chest and smiled like this was a game. Jess just seemed hurt.

"Why?" Anna asked.

"Business," Toby said. "Jack's right. We've got some shit to handle. We'll see you girls later? Tonight maybe?"

"I might host a party at *mi casa*," Max added.

Lizzie and Anna lit up at this, two little wind-up bimbo dolls. *Party, party, party.* Jess kicked at a stray bottle cap. I tried to tell her telepathically that this wasn't the right time, that she shouldn't be around for stuff like this, that she should go home and re-dye her hair because she was so beautiful and unique and so *Jess* before, and that she was too smart to hang out with wind-up dolls like Anna and Lizzie and losers like me and Toby and Max, and that if she got arrested I could never forgive myself.

But I knew my attempts at telepathy weren't working. Jess was frowning at me, waiting for me to tell the guys to let her and her friends stay.

She was only one month older than me, but ever since we'd met in third grade, she'd felt more like a little sister. Someone I needed to protect.

"Fine, we get the message," Jess said. She looped her arms around Anna's and Lizzie's. "See you around, boys."

The three of them finally headed back to the Shop N' Save. Jess kept glancing over her shoulder at me. I reached into my pocket, pulled out my phone, and texted her: *Sorry. Explain later.*

"Showtime," Toby said. Max was breathing faster now, clearing his throat and rubbing his hands together. I put my hand on his shoulder to steady him as the hideous orange SUV pulled up in front of us.

"Just stand watch and relax," I murmured in Max's ear. "Act natural. But not…you know, not *too* natural. Not nervous."

Max nodded. We watched Toby slip into the car as the driver eyed us suspiciously. He was a big guy, bulky, tattooed, with a shaved head and pierced eyebrows. His eyebrows were like lightning bolts across his brow, his jaw set in a grimace. A real stone grimace.

These were the kinds of guys that Toby and his cousins dealt with every day. These were the drug dealers I wanted far away from Jess.

And hopefully soon, away from me.

3

The kitchen smelled like a menthol ashtray.

Mom was at the table when I walked in, wearing her tattered lilac bathrobe, hair in a tangled mess. The radio was on, a talk show host murmuring the lotto. She tapped her cigarette against a clay ashtray on the table, my fumble-handed attempt at a great white shark during my 4th-grade obsession with oceanography. Wrinkles moved in the creases of her eyes as she squinted up at me.

"There you are," she said, voice filling with smoke as she took a long drag.

"Have you eaten?" I dropped my bag to the linoleum, nudged the dog's snout from going near my crotch, and opened the fridge. Nothing but milk, beer, and a few sad-looking radishes.

"Jesus, Mom, we need groceries," I said. I searched the cabinets for a scrap of something semi-nutritional for her to eat, but found only a stale pack of marshmallows and my stash of Lucky Charms. I made her a bowl.

Mom coughed deep from her chest and turned to the window. I opened the blinds to let the sunlight in and handed her the cereal. "Thanks, baby," she said, reaching up to lightly touch my cheek. Her fingers were freezing. "You've always been good to your mother."

"Where's Dad?" I asked. I leaned against the chair next to her and it wobbled unsteadily against my weight. I'd have to find the toolbox and fix it later.

"Oh, you know, the usual church-and-brewskis Sunday afternoon. Probably downing a six-pack with Joel and the boys."

"Great."

"Should be back soon," she said. She flicked her finger across her bubblegum-pink Bic, lighting another Menthol.

I put a hand on her shoulder and gave it a little rub. "Mom, you really shouldn't smoke so much. Remember what the doctor said?"

She laughed dryly, mussing her frizzy curls. Streaks of gray were pushing through the roots, licking up the last of her natural auburn.

"What for?" she asked dryly. "Fear of cancer, emphysema? I'm not afraid of dying. It's the living that fucks us over, babe. Remember that." She took a big, noisy bite of my cereal.

The front door banged opened and the smell of cheap beer, sweat, and something sour I could never quite pin down followed in the wake of my father. He kicked off his mud-coated boots and tossed the keys on the coffee table with a familiar clang. My stomach tied itself into a knot.

He strode over to smack me on the back a little too hard, like always. "Hey there, Jack, haven't seen you around lately."

"You either," I said.

Dad pushed past me to grab a beer from the fridge, snapped it open with the bottle opener clipped to his belt, and took a long swig. "You want one, son?" I shook my head and walked over to scratch the dog behind the ears. Old Gunther moaned and licked my palm.

"Has he been out?" I asked. My parents didn't respond, my father too busy thumbing through a thick wad of unpaid bills, Mom staring into the blue milk she stirred slowly around her bowl.

"I'll take him," I said aloud to no one in particular. As I clipped on Gunther's leash and reached for the doorknob, I heard them starting up again.

"You want to tell me what this bill is for, Ellie? Huh? You gonna pay this fucking bill anytime this century?"

"It's *my* money, Jim! I can buy whatever the hell I want with *my* money."

"The hell it's your money! Who do you think's been keeping a roof over your head? When's the last time you held down a job for more than two weeks straight?"

"*Three* weeks, for your information. And you shouldn't have opened my mail anyway. Federal offense, you know."

I heard my father sputter, imagining him gripping at his smelly old t-shirt like a slovenly cartoon character. "Federal offense? Goddamn it, Ellie, we're *married*!"

"Why don't you sit down a minute, Jim. You're raving drunk, for Christ's sakes."

"Federal fucking offense! Two wasted years of law school and you think you know every motherfucking—"

He's been drinking, he's been drinking, I told myself over and over as I stepped outside, inhaled the smell of lilacs and magnolia in the afternoon heat, and tugged Gunther down the road.

4

She was pissed at me. Like, big time pissed. Every time I said something, made a noncommittal remark, gestured, sighed, she just went "Mmhmm," and shrugged. She wouldn't look at me.

I hated this. Her bad mood was my bad mood. I had to snap her out of it before I lost it.

Jess and I walked past my house, then two blocks past hers, where her dad was probably smoking a cigar and trying to tune out the sounds of his sister's baby wailing day and night. I don't know how Jess got any sleep in there with her little cousin keeping her up at odd hours. I was about to ask her, but then I remembered she was giving me the silent treatment.

We went on these walks every Sunday. She'd come over to my house, knock on the door, listen to Mom's mumbo-jumbo for a few minutes, and then we'd be off without a word. Sometimes I'd fish around in Mom's purse for cash and bring her back a donut or a latte. I really wished she'd get out more.

We passed the Shop N' Save where I'd snubbed Jess

the other day, past the yogurt store where we'd worked last summer—or barely worked—blasting the dirtiest rap music imaginable when the manager wasn't there and lobbing chunks of fro-yo at each other while the customers gave us the stink eye. We lasted a month. I was happy to get fired. I hated the hats they made us wear, but Toby thought it was fucking hilarious, thought it made me look like a "professional fag." He always made a point to tell me so when he came in with Max or a group of bimbos from school. They laughed at me, wind-up doll hyenas with sharp fangs.

Worst of all, they laughed at Jess. Her cheeks burned the color of the raspberry sorbet and she threw her hat in the trash.

We passed the liquor store where a bum sat outside hustling for change. I dropped a quarter in his cup and he nodded at me. He was pretty young. I wondered where his parents were, if he had any. How he'd ended up without a place to crash in this dying town. Jess stopped in front of the tattoo place and stared inside the window. Since it was Sunday, closing time was soon, but we watched the work going on inside for a little while. A woman with long gray hair and wrinkles was getting a big black heart tattooed on her arm. A heart and the name CHARLES, written above it in thorny letters.

"Thinking of getting one?" I tried.

She put her hands in her shorts pockets. They were shorter than anything I'd ever seen her wear before. "Mmm," she said.

"Think she's a little old to be getting inked?" I asked. "Charles must be really special."

Jess popped her bubblegum.

Alrighty then.

I stared at our reflection in the shop window. You might have thought we were a couple, or maybe even brother and sister. We were about the same height, around the same build: lean, tall, with long torsos and heart-shaped faces. I'd read something in Mom's *Cosmo* about how you could determine your destiny from the shape of your face. I wondered what ours would be.

I was mumbling my thoughts to myself out loud. I quickly realized and cleared my throat, embarrassed even though I did this accidentally around Jess all the time.

"Who're you talking to, weirdo?" she asked. She was smiling.

"No one."

We stood like that for a while. I bumped her shoulder. She bumped me back.

The world righted itself in an instant.

"Look," I said. "I'm sorry about yesterday. I was a jerk for telling you and the girls to get lost. We were doing a deal, and I didn't want you involved. I—"

"It's not that," she said. "It's my mom. My dad wants me to stay with her this month while he helps with his sister with her new baby and everything. They're staying in my room until she gets her own place."

I knew that Jess's aunt was only nineteen. She had just given birth to a baby boy and had nowhere else to go. It was really nice of her dad, I thought. But Jess wasn't finished. She kicked at a stray bottle cap on the ground and it skittered across the pavement. "My mom's just been so irritated with me lately, like I can't do anything right," she went on. "Like I can't even breathe correctly. She actually criticized me for sighing too loudly, if you can believe it. She said, 'Jessica, who sighs like that? Knock it off!'"

I pictured Jess's hoity-toity mother, all decked out in cashmere and pearls and ironed slacks, even in the California heat. She wanted sunlit verandas to sit on and sip iced tea, country clubs with green, rolling hills, and a beach house on the "right" side of the country. She'd always shown way more interest in moving back to Massachusetts than spending time with her daughter. Except, she *had* loved Kellie, her favorite daughter.

Kellie Velez. The name was poison. *Danger. Don't think about it. Don't go there.*

I didn't. Instead, I put my hand on Jess's shoulder. "You want to get fro-yo and talk about it?"

She pressed her lips together. She desperately needed some Chapstick. Inside the tattoo parlor, the gray-haired lady was admiring her new ink. When she smiled, it was all gummy and pink because she had no teeth. I turned us both away from the window.

Jess let out a breath. "Fuck that yogurt place," she said, and we both laughed. "No, it's just…now I'm basically moving in with my mother. For a *month*."

"You mean in that gaudy hotel she lives in?"

"It's a *condominium building*," Jess said, making the word sound super, super hoity-toity. "And yeah, it's ugly. But Dad keeps telling me I have to try. He just keeps saying she's my mom and blah blah blah, custody agreement. Whatever. Legality is probably the only reason she agreed to it."

Living with Jess's mom would probably suck in some

ways, but it couldn't be worse than my house. Growing up, I'd spent so much time at the Velez residence that sometimes I thought I lived there. I used to lay in bed at night and pray I was a girl so I could sleep over there, or move in and become Jess's sister, but I never told her that.

Some secrets are best kept in that deep, dark corner of yourself.

We turned and started walking back into our neighborhood, all the one-story houses with dilapidated roofs and crumbling driveways, old people watching you from their porches, rocking back and forth in their chairs like time had stopped on this street. That was really the only thing left to do.

"Maybe it would be nice to get away from here for a while," I said. "She doesn't live that far."

"I'd have to take the county bus to school," Jess groaned. "I'm so used to Dad driving me. The bus is full of creepy homeless people and drug dealers."

I moved my tongue around my mouth so I wouldn't say anything. I hated when she said stuff like that.

"Maybe you should give her a chance," I said, even though I wasn't sure why I was saying it. "Maybe she really does love you and wants to show you that. The thing is, adults don't like to tell you stuff upfront, so you'll have to go there in person either way to find out. But isn't it better to know the truth?"

She stared at me for a while, frowning like I had just spoken some Martian language, like she couldn't quite figure me out. Then she broke into a grin and punched my arm.

"I *was* mad at you for yesterday, you punk," she said.

"But now that you gave me some decent advice, I'll let it slide."

I shrugged. "I do what I can. You want to smoke?"

She rolled her eyes. "I have to study, Jack. I have a big test tomorrow."

"But it's Sunday. Sundays are smoking days."

"Every day is a smoking day for you. You are such a stoner."

I laughed off her little jab like it didn't hurt.

"Shall we go to the Spot?" I asked.

The corner of her mouth turned up into a smile. "When have I ever said no the Spot, Jack?"

"The Spot solves everything."

She looped her arm through mine. "All of life's greatest quandaries are mysteriously solved the moment one sets foot in The Spot."

The Spot—*our* Spot—was just a patch of grassy bluff. It was overlooking the freeway—a strip of concrete glittering in the harsh sun—with the broad shoulders of those ever-looming mountains towering over it all. I loved it. We'd been going there since we'd first discovered it back in seventh grade, before the new housing developments and shopping center, back when it felt like this secret little retreat from the rest of Burro Hills.

Jess rested her head on my shoulder.

"What should we do now?" she asked. Her voice had that dreamy quality to it, and I knew we were about to play the game we always played whenever we sat at the Spot—the game where we dreamed of where we'd go and what we'd do when we finally got out of here. When we were younger, it was Disney World or Six Flags or the world's biggest indoor splash park. When we got a little older, it got a little vaguer, a little more out of reach.

What should we do now? The question fell from her mouth and rolled out across the land below us, into the sounds of honking horns and revving engines, and the air that was always thick with exhaust fumes. "Let's just get a car and get out of here," she said. "We'll drive down the Pacific Highway and never look back. What do you think?"

"That sounds sick," I said. "But I don't know. Are you paying for gas? I'm dead broke."

She laughed. "Don't think about the money. The money doesn't exist in the fantasy. We can go anywhere we want. We could run from here, just run away and do whatever we liked. We could see the country, maybe see the world. There's so much more outside this town. So much more besides high school and college and some boring nine-to-five job we'll get someday and totally hate."

We. She'd go to college. *She'd* get the nine-to-five. I wouldn't go anywhere.

But I closed my eyes and imagined it anyway, just for a moment. The fantasy of us she'd created. Us away from everywhere. All of this. Together.

"But you'll leave anyway," I said. Behind my eyelids, the vision popped and deflated like a sad balloon. "You're going to college for sure. And you're probably going out-of-state."

"That's not necessarily true," she said, but she said it quietly, and we both knew that it was. Jess had always dreamed of attending an Ivy—or even a Little Ivy, if they'd have her. She had the grades, the family connections, the money. She could do it. She could make it.

What the hell did I have?

I would stay here, and I would probably die here. But at least for another year, we'd be together in this broken, crumbling town, rotting and burning to death in the baking sun.

Or, we could just say "fuck it" and make that fantasy real. We could go out there now, drive a thousand miles before crashing into the stars…like we were alive, like we were invincible, laughing until we wanted to cry.

We would open our eyes and it would be beautiful, all of it, and the world would crack open and arms would reach out for us and we'd finally be home. We'd strip our skins and run right into the light, into a future of possibility and fresh air and freedom, real freedom, the freeway flayed by our tires as we drove over this place and never looked back. All of it would be gone, Toby, his cousins, Mom, Dad, the boys, the girls, Burro Hills…all those watchful mountains looming in our rearview mirrors.

I clung to this vision as we watched the sunlight catch on the tires of the hundreds of cars on the freeway, going somewhere, anywhere, someplace better than this.

And I thought, if only for a moment: *She's getting out. I'm not. Maybe there's nothing left for me to do but run.*

5

I was only thirteen.

I told myself that over and over whenever the memory would spring into my mind and attack me, in an otherwise peaceful moment, when I was going about my day, minding my own business.

It was a very Velez Christmas party. Their modest little ranch house had been transformed, dolled up with tinsel, blow-up Santa Clauses, and snowmen. A big plastic Christmas tree was planted in the middle of the living room, shedding cheap ornaments. Jess played with her cousins, chasing them around the house while her mom poured glass after glass of champagne and complained to her husband about how her youngest daughter was getting too old to act like a boy.

The way she said it made me feel sick inside my stomach.

I sat on their gold-and-green striped couch in the living room, busying myself with my Gameboy, the murmur and laughter of adults drunk on wine and Christmas spirit creating a peaceful white noise barrier. Any minute now, Jess would tire of her games and come find me, and we'd crawl upstairs to her room and whisper our thoughts about all the grown-ups around us.

Any minute now.

But the minutes lingered on and turned to hours, and soon I was wandering the house, bored, bumping past adults and sneaking flutes of champagne and handfuls of frosted sugar cookies until my stomach ached. The noise and the food and the clatter of silverware were starting to give me a headache too, so I climbed upstairs and lay down in Jess's bedroom, snuggling up in her big purple comforter.

The door opened with a creak. It was dark in the room and in the hallway, and for a moment, relief flooded through me.

"Jess!" I said. "Thank God, I was so bored down there. Do you—"

But it wasn't Jess. It was her big sister Kellie, her big sister about to go off to the University of Southern California and join a sorority and get a job that would make her rich and even more popular. Her big sister with the long, platinum blonde hair, the too-tight sweater, the giant fake boobs, the crispy orange tan. I stiffened.

"What do you want?" I asked.

She laughed, a little musical laugh that made me want to pull the covers up over my head. "Oh Jack, why are you always so upset to see me?"

She stumbled over to me, the way Dad always did after he'd had too many beers. She sat down on the bed and yanked the comforter off me, revealing my scrawny body engulfed by a hoodie. I said nothing.

"You're such a cute little guy," she slurred, reaching over and tracing my cheek with her fingertip. "You're gonna be a looker someday. Trust me, all the girls will want you."

I shrugged. Kellie groaned, mumbled something about it being "so hot in here," then moved to take off her sweater.

"Don't!" I said, but she'd already lifted it over her head, revealing her big, bulging watermelon boobs. She wasn't wearing a bra.

She cocked her head at me and squeezed at her tits, at the pink, pointed nipples. "What's wrong?" Her voice was all weird and husky. "You haven't seen my new breasts yet, have you?"

I couldn't speak. My mouth was sewn shut and my stomach had turned to ice. I tried to avert my eyes, to look anywhere but directly at her chest. She'd shown me them before, when I'd hung out at Jess's house one night and she'd been all tipsy and handsy. But that time, I'd managed to get away, make up some excuse about how Jess was calling for me in another room. I'd managed to evade her.

"These were real expensive, you know," Kellie said. Her breath smelled sour and strong, like Daddy's before he got angry. I started shaking. "What's wrong? Don't like boobs? What, are you a little faggot or something? You must be a little faggot." I'd never seen her like this, so cruel and detached from her body. "Everybody loves me. All of you want me. You just don't know it yet, you're so young and..."

And Kellie reached forward and pulled my face to hers. The shaking got worse, so bad I thought I might collapse into myself. She touched her lips gently to mine—sweet, sticky, lip gloss-covered lips—then pressed them hard against my mouth, hungry, angry.

She pushed me against the bed and tugged at the seams of my pants. *No*, I thought. I tried to say it, but her mouth was crushing mine. My arms had gone limp at my sides. My body refused to move. My heart was two fists pumping at my chest, screaming for help.

She reached down into my pants, under my boxers, and touched my dick. It remained limp in her cold hand. She tried to awaken it, tried to get it to move, but it was frozen solid like the rest of me. She stopped kissing and frowned at me like I was defective, like I had deeply insulted her.

"Kellie? You up here, honey?" It was Mrs. Velez's voice, climbing up through the shadows and into the room. My chest loosened a little. Kellie cursed and pushed me away, scrambling to get her sweater back on, then wiped her mouth and spit right onto Jess's clean carpet. She didn't even look at me as she left.

"Little faggot," was all I heard her say.

I curled into a ball and waited for my mom to come and get me. I curled up inside of myself and went somewhere very far away, somewhere where no one could ever touch me again.

6

It was hot, so hot that you could smell the tar burning on the streets, that smoldering rubber tire smell. We stripped off our sweat-soaked shirts and sneakers and sat beneath the shade of an aging sycamore.

"Not even a fucking breeze and it's only April," Max grumbled. "Con, hand me that, man."

Connor tossed him the big water bottle. Max drained it over his head, cool water streaming down his neck and back. My skin itched with envy.

Connor lit a joint, passed it around. He seemed perfectly content even in this sweltering haze, lying against the tree, one hand behind his head, legs stretched out. He took a long drag and blew smoke rings into the air. I sat by him and tried to simulate his body language, to let my head just rest against the trunk. It scratched at my neck but felt better this way, not fighting the heat, just letting it burn through me, letting go.

He passed me the joint and exhaled. I felt the smoke hit my cheek.

"Look at those fucking fags," Toby said. He spat into the street, gesturing at a group of kids popping open a fire hydrant, squealing with joy and running in circles as a torrent of water spurted up and splashed down on them, turning the street into a splash park.

Connor's lips twitched into a smile. "I don't know, man, I like the way they think."

"Yeah, but look at 'em," Toby said. "Look at those pansy-ass BMXs. Probably cost Mommy and Daddy a good grand. Bet they can't even do a fire hydrant." He grabbed the joint out of my hand.

Connor laughed, shook his hair out of his eyes. "They're like twelve, dude. Besides, they're fucking with the right kind of fire hydrant."

"It *is* hot as balls, Tobe," Max said.

Toby sat up and spat again. A thick ball of saliva landed right by Connor's feet. "Then why don't you go fucking play with them?"

Connor stood. "Thinking about it." His hand reached out to me, beckoning towards me. "Come on, Jack."

The guys were sitting there like bacon in a frying pan, moaning and hawking spit, and then there was Connor, the sun hitting his olive skin. I took his hand and let him help me up. He smiled at me and I smiled back.

Toby growled an insult and Max snapped something back at him, but I couldn't hear them when we hit the opened fountain, the sound of rushing water that filled my ears and licked my skin clean and cold. Connor laughed with his head back, mouth wide open, catching the water on his tongue. We ran around the hydrant like little twelve-year-old fags, the boys at the tree dissolving into smoke.

7

I hated Burro Hills High, with its ugly orange lockers and dirty floors and halls that smelled like a bad mix of cleaning solution, smoke, and something foul. I hated the vile graffiti written all over the stalls, endless webs connecting names to people who'd fucked, and who was fighting who, and who the rival groups were. Jess would always tell me stories about the girl's bathroom, the peeling paint and the names of girls we'd gone to elementary school with, things like "cunt" and "dirty whore" written in magic marker next to their names. It was quietly sinister, a warning to toe the line and know your place and hang with your crowd or you'd be marked next.

I especially hated it on days like this, when it was swarming with cops. They were everywhere, patrolling the front of the school, the courtyard, the classrooms, their walkie-talkies crackling and beeping. The pigs brought a menace with them, something we could all feel as they stepped across our hallways and peeked inside our classrooms.

"It's getting worse," I said. Jess nodded. We were at lunch, standing by the water fountain near the entrance to the courtyard in the aftermath of a fight. One freshman girl and her crew had shouted insults at a senior girl, and soon fists were flying and hair was being pulled. One of the seniors, a tiny girl named Tasha, had a busted upper lip, but kept calm and collected while she was questioned by the cops. Rumor had it that she'd slammed a freshman so hard into the vending machine that two Cokes had popped out.

They say girls fight with their words, not their fists.

They've clearly never been to Burro Hills High. Fights were our circus sideshows, our sick distractions. Everyone would pop out their phone and film the action, pushing and shoving to get a better look.

"I could really use a smoke right now," I said.

"*Now*? Are you joking?"

I shrugged. "If we go by the tennis courts…come on, Jess, Andrew's here today. He's got our back."

Andrew was one of Toby's cousins, a clean-cut cop who often patrolled the school. He and his partner, a young guy fresh out of community college, always turned a blind eye to Toby and his friends' boozing and drugging. He was also probably the reason we never heard about any of the cousins on the nightly news.

"Why can't you just wait to get home to smoke?" Jess whined. "Are you that addicted to weed that you need a hit every half-hour?"

It annoyed me so fucking much whenever she said that, like I was some hopeless addict who was constantly stoned. I wanted to tell her off, but she was grinning at me so innocently that she must have been joking. I reached over and ruffled her hair. "You don't get it, Jess. It's okay that you don't get it."

She rolled her eyes. "Oh, so I can't possibly understand your stoner predilections?"

I sighed. "I'm heading over there now," I said. "You can come or you can watch this freshman mess."

"One of the girls is a senior."

"Whatever."

I hesitated for a moment. Part of me wanted to walk with her down those halls like we used to, talking and laughing and making fun of the mayhem at this school. But with the crowd that had gathered, still simmering with energy of the recent fight…it all made me too jumpy. I needed something to take the edge off, a quiet place to sit and think.

"Okay," Jess said, her back turned to me as she surveyed the continuing chaos. She twirled her hair around her fingers nervously. "Whatever. I'll see you later, I guess."

Come with me, I almost said again, and I felt like such an asshole, because instead, I patted her arm and made my way down that ugly orange hallway with its peeling lockers and sharp smells of ammonia. Day in and day out we were herded through these doors, mindless cattle told to sit and pay attention and study and work hard so one day we could have a bright future in a cold office building that smelled of ammonia, where we'd pay attention and work hard day in and day out.

Go figure.

I had a vision of Jess and I stealing a car and driving east, just hitting the country roads, watching the expanse of sky roll over us as the world opened up, wide open space all around. Every time I got this itch to run, to drive, to leave, I had to smoke a little to keep myself from flying off the handle.

Because I knew, even if I did steal that car and go, she would never in a million years actually come with me.

I'd be getting really, really stoned today.

8

"I admit it, I'm just a thirsty virgin," said Max.

The boys and I were sitting behind the gym at lunch, far enough away from security so we could smoke undetected. It was also a prime viewing spot for girls outside at gym class, girls in field hockey skirts or tiny running shorts. And for the first time, Connor was joining us.

"I feel you, man," Toby said, appraising a particularly busty brunette who had just scored a goal. "Except, wait, I'm not a virgin. Oops."

"Well I am, and it fucking sucks," Max said.

"Don't worry, dude," Connor said. "When you're the CEO of the next pharmaceutical empire, I'm sure you'll get plenty of tail."

"And we'll fix your problem," Toby said, putting an arm around Max. "We'll find you someone hot, give you pointers. Am I right, Jack?"

"Uh, sure," I said.

"I mean, Jack's not a virgin. Right?" Toby asked. All of them turned to me.

I hesitated before choosing an answer. "No, of course not."

Connor snorted a laugh.

"What?" I said. "What's so funny about that?"

"Nothing," Connor grinned, locking eyes with me. He flicked the ashes of his cigarette in the direction of Toby's shoes. "It's not the least bit amusing."

"Well give us some details!" Max said.

"What is this, a fucking slumber party?" I said. "Why do you pervs want to know so much?"

"We're just curious, man," Max said. "Who've you been with? Anyone we know?"

Toby leaned in and hissed in Max's ear, "I bet he's fucked Jess."

"Oooh!" Max snickered.

"Shut up!" I said. "You guys are nasty. Jess is like my sister."

"A sister I wouldn't mind getting friendly with," Toby said. "She's sexy as hell. Come on, you must have at least thought about it."

I shrugged and pulled out my cigarettes, putting one between my lips and fumbling for a lighter. Connor held one out in front me, and I let him light me up, let that sweet smoke fill my lungs and calm my nerves.

"I don't fuck and tell," I said.

"Bullshit!" Toby said. "You must have. There's no possible way. You're with her like all the time."

"Yeah, you have thought about it, haven't you?" said Max.

"You've gotta be gay not to," Toby laughed.

"Maybe," I said, "Maybe I have. And you'll never know."

Toby cackled and batted Max's arm. "He's so fucked her."

"Definitely," Max agreed. "What about you, Connor?"

"Have I fucked Jess?"

"No, man, who've you been with here?"

Connor shrugged. "I don't fuck and tell."

"Whatever," Max said. "We've heard all about you. You get around, bro."

He just smiled and stood up, stomping out his cigarette. "I've got shit to do. You kids have fun with your gossip. I'll see you later." I watched him walk away, wishing I could just get up like that and leave when the guys were pissing me off. I wondered if he really was who everyone was blowing him up to be.

The next day, he touched my hand.

It was momentary, a blink-and-you'll-miss-it kind of deal. At first, I thought I'd imagined it, that light succession of taps—one, two, three—that lingered for a moment on the surface of my skin.

I was sitting in World History, completely engrossed in the in-class essay we were writing, and I guess he was there to drop something off for our teacher because by the time I felt it and looked up, he was already on his way out the door.

I got a kind of chill, a secret thrill that I held onto for the rest of the day. I laughed more at Toby's dumbass jokes, at Max's poor imitations of girls. I even kept patient while Jess complained to me about the latest crisis in the never-ending saga that was her life.

But by the time I'd made it home to find Gunther whining for his dinner and Mom curled up on the couch in her robe, snoring, a bottle of half-empty gin on the coffee table, the magic had faded from those sacred places on my knuckles.

As I stood watching Mom snore softly, Gunther's cold wet nose against my legs, a strange sort of déjà vu flashed through my mind, like something buried deep in the sand. It was this weird feeling that was poking at the back of my brain, and it didn't leave me even after I'd fed Gunther and left the house to take a walk down the street.

Then I got the text from Toby.

"My house tonight. Six. Be there, motherfucker."

I hated Toby's house. It was crumbling and dark, all creaking floorboards and antique furniture that felt heavy and sickly.

At least, that's how I'd remembered it from all those years ago. Toby and I had met in fifth grade when he'd tried to steal my skateboard, and I'd shoved him in the mud so hard he'd scraped his knee up bad. When he saw the blood, his pink face had scrunched up like a fist and then he'd started cackling like it was the funniest thing in the whole world. He laughed so hard that snot came out of his nose, and that just made the whole thing even funnier. We've been friends ever since.

My phone bleeped again. "Never mind," it read. "Meet at seven. My fucking relatives are here."

Toby's relatives were always dropping by unannounced, making sure his cousins who frequented the decaying home had enough to eat now that his parents were dead and gone. The relatives were always giving, smiling with their mouths but never their eyes, and if they noticed the rank stench of weed or the group of tattooed men measuring and weighing bags of cocaine and crack now and then in the kitchen, they never said a thing. Tony's club owner uncle never really came by much. Usually he was there to collect his monthly cut of the profit.

The rest of the relatives came by every week or so, bringing flowers that smelled like furniture wax, root beer, and little Tupperware containers of potato salad and mac and cheese, whispering in hushed voices and worried tones as they hurried out as soon as their gifts were accepted.

Toby would leave the food in the fridge to rot. His oldest cousin, D'Angelo, was his official guardian, but I rarely saw him around. I preferred it that way.

Thinking of his house made me shiver. I wrote back, "Should I invite Connor?"

Not more than three seconds later he responded, "As long as he brings some good shit."

Toby's creepy house was really only good for several things: Drugs, booze, and a loud, pounding bass.

And the thought of Connor being there…it brought back that secret thrill from before.

When I got to Toby's, he, Max and his cousin Gabriel were already seated in the living room. It was always so weird seeing burly, tattooed guys like that on all that flowery, antique furniture. We used to hang out in this room as kids, watching Saturday morning cartoons and eating cereal so sugary it made my teeth hurt. Now the walls were yellowed with smoke fumes, the sandy carpet covered in beer and soda stains, and the flowery sofas and chairs afflicted with cigarette burns.

"No, see, Ambien is not a benzodiazepine, nor is it a hallucinogen. It's a hypnotic," Max was explaining as I walked in, doodling chemicals in his notebook.

"But you can get fucked up off it, right? Like hallucinate and shit?" asked Gabriel. I put my bag down and joined them on the flower couch with the cigarette burns.

"Well no, you'd probably just fall asleep," said Max. "See, it's similar to a benzo in that it…Oh hey, Jack."

"Am I interrupting something?"

"Just business," said Toby, and as usual I couldn't tell if he was joking or not. He was seated directly across from us in a wingback chair that used to be something beautiful, but now was browning around the edges. "You bring me anything good?"

"Nah," I said. "Connor said he would, though."

"Who the fuck is Connor?" Gabriel asked.

"A friend of ours," I said quickly. "He's cool. He goes to school with us."

Gabriel shook his head. "Nah man, he may be cool but he can't know about our business. And he can't come in here. You didn't tell him anything, Toby, did you?"

"No, no way," Toby said. "He's straight, right, Jack?"

"What?"

Toby looked at me like I might be a moron. "I said he's cool, right?"

"Yeah," I said. "Yeah, yeah, he's cool."

Gabriel swung his hand across the coffee table, knocking a glass to floor. It shattered instantly, shards of glass nearly puncturing Max's arm. I heard him gasp as Gabriel got up in Toby's face and shoved him, hard.

"You don't say anything to him, you got that? You keep your fucking mouth shut. That goes for you and your punk ass friends." For the first time in a long time, I saw fear in Toby's eyes. "You remember what D'Angelo said, yeah?"

It was then that the doorbell rang.

By then Gabriel was already on his way out the back, Toby trailing after him. I could hear the shouting, the cursing and the grumbling and growling that slowly picked up in volume.

I opened the front door to let Connor in. Just the sight of him made my chest tighten.

"Hey," he said, glancing around the room at the broken

glass and Max all backed up in the corner, spooked. "Did I miss the party?"

"Uh, screw the party, man," I heard myself say, glancing over my shoulder to make sure Toby and Gabriel were out of earshot. "We're actually gonna head down to the Strip now."

"We are?" Max piped up. He had gotten over his brief state of shock and was now standing in the middle of the room, swaying back and forth, hands in his pockets. "I thought we were gonna chill here."

"Max," I said through gritted teeth, turning to shoot him a look. "Shut up."

Connor just grinned and pushed past me, making his way into the house before I could stop him. "Interesting digs." He pulled a joint from his pocket. "Got a light, Max?"

Max turned to me for guidance, but I just shrugged and sat down on the ratty old flower couch. Clearly no one was listening to me.

Connor sat toking away, sitting cross-legged on the floor and regaling Max with tales of his past life as a pot dealer. Was this kid for real? I could usually read people inside and out like a pamphlet, see if they were full of shit or not right away, but Connor was like some dense tomb that I couldn't interpret.

I kept looking over my shoulder, waiting for Gabriel—or worse, D'Angelo—to pop back into the room. I kept wondering where the fuck Toby had gone, when he was coming back. If Toby was with us in the house, things were cool. But if Toby left the room…

Ever since Toby's parents had croaked, things had gotten extra bonkers around here. You never knew when a pot might boil over, so to speak, and Gabriel had been on edge all morning. Even before snapping at Toby, he'd been pacing a lot, glowering at various pieces of furniture, mumbling to no one and nothing in particular.

Something was up in the family business.

But Connor seemed so comfortable there, so not ready for things to pop off. Inviting Connor here had been such a bad idea, and I cursed myself for not thinking ahead to a situation like this one.

"I'm bored," I said. "Come on, let's go to…to the mall." *Shit.* It was the first and only thing I could think of.

Max frowned. "The *mall*?" he asked incredulously. Connor just laughed and took another hit on his joint, passing it to me. I felt myself grow red and put a hand up, declining. I needed to be sober when shit hit the fan.

I needed to think of better things to say.

"Or we could go to that new arcade on Jane Street," I offered, feeling dumber than ever. *Arcade?* What were we, ten?

"You okay, dude?" Max asked. He was getting high, his eyes glazed over and his voice light and dreamy. "Just relax. Take a hit."

Connor cocked his head at me, as if trying to figure out why I kept cracking my knuckles over and over like I was playing some twisted version of the accordion.

"Oh," was all I heard. I looked up from the couch and saw where it came from. "Oh well, okay now," the voice said.

D'Angelo stood in the entrance to the living room.

Fuck.

D'Angelo was huge, a bear of a man, pushing forty

and sporting a full chest of hair, a thick beard and a shaved head. Prison tattoos ran up and down his meaty arms. He wore dark pants, a fitted black work shirt, and steel-toed boots. A silver apron hung over his clothes, covered in something dusty and white.

They were cooking out back. I could smell it on him, that sharp, diesel scent Toby sometimes wore and badly tried to cover up with body spray.

"What's up, man?" Connor asked, in that lilting, boyish tone of his. "Want a hit?" Fuck, was he was serious?

"We were just leaving," I said, forcing a shrug. "We won't bother you." I stood and started walking to the front door, nodding at the guys to follow me.

But neither Max nor Connor moved. D'Angelo licked his lips and leaned against the living room doorframe, leering at them. At Connor in particular.

"No thanks, man, I don't partake anymore," D'Angelo said to Connor. His voice was like the groan of a motor. "I'm just curious what you boys are up to, hanging out inside our house on a beautiful day like this. I don't believe we've had the pleasure of meeting." He held out his hand to Connor, and that idiot stood and took it.

"Connor Orellana," he said. Full name. *Idiot.* "Nice to meet you, man. I moved here from Creek Way earlier this year."

"D'Angelo," said The Monster of the Miller Residence. He smiled slowly at Connor, revealing a mouthful of silver-capped teeth. "Long-time resident. Very long." Then he laughed, a garbled guttural noise that made me want to puke.

"We have to go, guys," I said. "That thing we have to

go to is uh, starting soon." Max seemed to understand by now, and had made his way to my side. He'd met D'Angelo once or twice before, and none of those meetings had ended well. But Connor seemed transfixed by the giant Miller cousin, who was squinting at him like a scientist might a new species of beetle.

"What's the hurry?" D'Angelo asked, still staring at Connor. He was taking in his fitted tank top, his board shorts, his taut shoulder muscles, devouring the sight of him. "I think I have a right to know who's in my house, learn a little bit about each new guest. Especially such an interesting one. And an *unexpected* one."

"Connor," I said. My voice had gone dark.

D'Angelo took a long breath. My heart bounced around. He nodded at me, as if I were directly responsible for Connor being here. Which I was. "You guys stay out of here from now on, alright? This is a family business. This is not *the arcade on Jane Street*." I shivered. He'd been listening to our conversation. Fucking creep. "Got it?"

I nodded dumbly, and then he slunk off, disappearing back into the kitchen, but not before turning and leering at Connor in a way that made my blood run cold.

"What the fuck was that about?" Connor asked when we got outside.

I shook my head. "Nothing."

"He's kind of…well, kind of in charge in that family," Max explained. "He's uh…Jack?"

I shrugged. "It's nothing, really."

Connor laughed and reached into his pocket for another joint. "I think he had the hots for me or something."

I surprised myself by how fast and hard I grabbed his

wrist and stopped him in his tracks. "Don't go near him ever again. I'm serious." Max stopped walking.

"Okay man," Connor said. He patted my elbow until I released my vice grip, the breath I didn't realize I'd been holding in. "I won't. I got it."

"To the Strip?" Max asked nervously.

I nodded, turning away from them so they wouldn't see the look on my face. "Yeah. Sure. To the Strip."

9

At night, the Strip came alive. During the day it was just another shitty part of town, a run-down street with cracks in the sidewalks and greasy corner stores like The Pharmacy, which sold Adderall, weed, and designer drugs to the neighborhood kids and junkies if you knew who to ask. Bums and heroin addicts lingered, shooting up and begging for change, shaking their coins around in their tin cups…the musical clatter of San Juan Boulevard. The guys and I only went there to get weed and booze from the shops that didn't card. It was creepy in the daylight.

Once we were walking around there around noon and a short little guy with a scrunched-up face stopped us, gesturing for us to see his wares. About a dozen kitchen knives were carefully laid out on a little fleece blanket. "Nice present for your *abuela*," he'd said, gesturing to the knives. His left eye was bulging out of his socket and twitching profusely. Max tugged on my arm to keep walking, but I'd felt his stare follow me all the way down the street.

There were a few tacky clothing places and coffee shops that catered to the locals on the Strip, with bizarre characters like the man who wore a python around his neck, and the woman who wandered up and down the road, cradling a plastic baby doll in her arms. She was always humming and staring straight ahead at something the rest of us couldn't see.

But at night, all the creeps and weirdos seemed to fall into the background. That's when the Strip lit up in a million neon candy-colored lights, when the bars opened and the crowds filled in, high school kids and twenty-somethings, the occasional sugar daddies looking for their next fix. We hung out there a lot at night, a good place to smoke up as long as you knew where the cops were. They'd hired a lot of young asshole guys on the force around that time, big tough-boys fresh out of community college who liked to push people around and make a big scene. As long as you steered clear of them, you were usually good.

Toby's creepy uncle owned Bazingo, the nightclub with the flashing marquee outside that pumped out rap and dance music and drunken, sloppy fights into the streets. Connor, Max and I got in with little more than a quick glance at our fakes. Pretty girls in tight skirts and stilettos drank fruity cocktails, grinding on the stripper poles in the center of the dance floor. Men huddled around, leering at their half-naked bodies over cups of pale ale and Bud Light. The guys and I had brought Jess and her friends once, against our better judgment. When they arrived they instantly had stars in their eyes, chattering excitedly, so thrilled to be in a *real-life nightclub.* They let all the older men and frat stars feel them up until Toby bought them a round of shots, then another, and another. They got so drunk they spent the night puking in the Pepto Bismol pink bathroom stalls that smelled like urine and something that had died forty years ago. Toby and Max went to creep on college girls while I took turns holding Jess and Anna and Lizzie's hair, rubbing their backs as they retched and vomited every ounce of liquor till their stomachs were raw.

Sometimes I just couldn't stand it, that ache that I felt deep inside my chest, that utterly hopeless feeling that crept into my head and bogged me down day after day. High school was monotony, repetitive, dull. They said the real world would be harder, more intense, less forgiving. Would I end up moving on after school, leaving this shitty town and never looking back, or would I become some drug addict, some deadbeat on the Strip peddling for loose change?

Sometimes the only thing I wanted was neon club lights and a thumping bass, cheap liquor in my system that worked like engine fuel. Bazingo was the place to do it, the place where you could snort some lines behind the counter with the bartenders and let the hollow sound of the music swallow you whole. It was easy to see how you could escape into all of that, how you could go into that world and never come out.

Connor loved the Strip the first time he came with us that night in April. Of course he did. He loved the lights, the girls, the action. Me, him, and Max drank warm beers wrapped in brown paper bags, watched the hookers in tight skirts waiting for tricks in the loop-de-loop, their pimps watching from the shadows. I knew for a fact that Toby had slept with at least three of them. I wondered what kind of

STIs he had. Toby didn't answer any of my texts or calls. We hadn't heard from him since Gabriel broke that glass and D'Angelo creeped on Connor. I hoped that he was fine, just busy cooking with his cousins. Or even better, getting some sleep.

Connor loved Bazingo, too. That night he met a redhead who was so drunk she could barely speak, and hung all over him throughout the night while I did shot after shot of Fireball to drown it all out. We all stumbled home to Max's house, a peaceful place with nice parents who let Connor and I crash on the couch and the floor. They even brought us blankets. I fell asleep drunk and dizzy on a white shaggy rug, the living room tilting slowly, Connor's arm just inches away from mine, the static between our skin electric.

10

Toby texted me bright and early the next morning, when I was sound asleep on Max's floor.

Meet me at Albert's at 10. Business meeting.

I found him there, holed up at Albert's Diner on Jane Street, high as a kite, eyes darting around in circles like a dog chasing its tail and drinking black coffee. Bad sign.

"You wanted to meet me?" I asked. I sat in the booth across from him. The jazz music that played from the diner's tinny speakers and the hustle and bustle of waitresses and hungry patrons made this a good place to have this kind of a conversation.

Toby sniffed loudly and wiped his nose on his sleeve. He was wearing the same green long-sleeve from yesterday. "Sorry I vanished yesterday, dude. Family stuff. But listen, we need to do more deals. Business is booming." He was talking fast, slurping coffee after every other sentence.

I nodded and signaled for a waitress, ordered him a plate of eggs and bacon. Now was as good a time as any. "Listen, Tobe, about that—"

"My cousins are putting mad pressure on me, man. I have to sell my share by the end of the month or I'm out of the business. I *cannot* be out of the business." He tapped the table with his finger so I hard I thought he might bruise it. "So I need your help. No more Max at the drop-off spots. He's a liability. Connor could probably handle the look-out position better, anyway. D'Angelo likes him, said that he'd fit in well with—"

"No," I said.

He frowned at me, slowing down for the first time in that whole conversation to take a full breath. "No, what?"

"No, Connor," I said. "And I'm out too. I can't do these deals anymore, Tobe. I just can't."

Toby started nodding and flexing his fingers, staring out the window. When his eggs and bacon arrived, he didn't touch them.

"More coffee," he told the waitress, not even bothering to look at her.

I put on my hand on his wrist. "You've had enough, dude."

"Don't tell me when I've had enough, Jack!" he snapped. He said it loudly enough for the whole restaurant to turn around and stare at us.

I lowered my voice. "You're tweaking, bro. How much blow did you do last night, anyway? That shit's not good for you. Look, we've had this conversation before. I know it's your family and your business and all, but I can't risk doing this anymore. I'm out, okay?"

Toby stared at his eggs. "Give me a reason."

"I don't need a reason, Toby. I said no."

"Give me a good reason. You're not going to college. Your parents are deadbeats. You have no other job prospects when school's over. You get free weed and discounted blow. So give me one good reason why you're ditching me here."

If anyone else said this to me, I'd deck them, knock them out cold. But Toby was different. I knew where he was coming from, why he was the way he was. And he knew me pretty well, better than any friend besides Jess ever had. So I didn't even think of getting mad.

Until he said what he said.

"I know why. It's because you're a pussy."

The word snapped a rubber band inside of me. "What did you say?"

He leaned in closer across the table, sniffling loudly. "You're a little *pussy*, Jack, and that's why you're shit scared of—"

But before he could finish, I reached across the table and yanked him by the shirt collar, pulling him close to me. Plates and dishes clanked and rattled. I could feel the entire restaurant's attention pinned to us. Toby's sour coffee breath was in my face. The jazz music had stopped.

"Don't. Ever. Call. Me. That. Again," I said. "I'm out. You understand, Toby?"

He just nodded, staring at me like he was seeing me for the first time. I'd never spoken to him like that before.

I let him go, and he fell back against the headboard. I dashed out of the restaurant, the sun hitting me full in the face, my hands shaking so badly I could barely hold the handlebars as I biked home. The anger pumped through my blood as I pedaled, harder and harder until my legs felt like they might give out.

Something inside of me was stirring, awakening. I needed to smoke so bad. I needed to crawl into a hole and scream.

It hadn't always been like this between us. There was a time when we were younger and dumber and the world wasn't as scary and his parents were still alive, back when his house was warm and bright and sounded like their laughter and smelled like their cooking. Real cooking, no diesel fumes and cocaine. Toby and I would stay up late into the night playing video games, making forts out of sheets in his room and going on exploratory missions in his basement, sieving through boxes and cartons and layers of Miller family secrets coated in dust.

We were thirteen when Toby's parents were hit by a drunk driver, slamming into them at nearly 100 mph while they were merging off the freeway. They were only a mile away from their house, and just a few more from where they both worked. They died almost instantly in the crash. The driver suffered severe head trauma, went into a coma or something.

Toby stopped speaking for a month. Just went completely mute. Then a few of his cousins moved in, D'Angelo and Toby's other uncle, the one who never told us his name, and they were around all the time.

Toby only started speaking again because of me. I'd tried for weeks to get him to say something. I'd tried to lure him in by writing him funny poems or drawing cartoons of the two of us committing mild acts of mayhem. I'd tried biking to his house every morning to take the bus with him to school. He kept his face stoic and wore sunglasses a lot, even indoors. The teachers let him get away with it because he was a poor orphan boy.

Then one evening, when the crickets were out and playing a dusk-time lullaby, Toby wrote me a note and put it in my mailbox—writing notes was the only way he'd communicate, and only with me—inviting me over to his house. It was empty for once, his cousins and uncle out doing God knows what. It was the first time I'd been over there since the funeral. The rooms inside the house were heavy, each one feeling as though rain had soaked right through them. So we went outside and sat on the sloping hill in his backyard that was overgrowing with weeds and flanked by giant pines. An ominous brown shed that had once been home to our adventures stood at the bottom of the slope, a place I had now been banned from entering by the new Miller men of the house. Sometimes it smelled like diesel fuel, but Toby wouldn't tell me why.

"They were killed by some reckless asshole," Toby said. I almost jumped out of my shorts, I was so surprised to hear his voice. It sounded deeper and fuller than I'd last remembered. "Who dies just a mile away from their house?"

Toby's parents ran the old auto repair shop three miles up the road from where they lived, the one that they'd been so excited to take over after his grandfather left it to them. They were there night and day, always coming home smelling like diesel fumes, always talking about who to fire or hire next, how to cut costs and keep things running smoothly. How to keep the business going strong and still save up enough to send Toby to college.

Something in Toby's face broke, and for the first time in forever, he started crying. I had to slap my arm to remind myself that this was real.

"Grandpa left them that place before he died, and they were so happy," Toby sobbed. "And now they're gone, and Grandpa's gone, and everything here is dying."

I touched his shoulder. "You're not dying, Toby."

He jerked away from me like my hands were made of hot coals. "Don't touch me!" Then he spat angrily into the grass. "Maybe I should be dying! I want to die! I deserve to die. Why should they die, and I stay here? It isn't fair!"

He got up and ran to the house. I called after him, but he locked the door and refused to let me in, even when I banged on all the windows. I had to hop the fence to get to my bike.

Two days later, Toby called me up like nothing had been wrong, like we'd never had this conversation and I hadn't seen him bawling like a baby.

He said he was part of this new family business venture, a cool new way to make some money. One that was easy money.

He asked me if I wanted in.

11

Toby sulked for a few days about me leaving the business, ignored a bunch of my texts and calls. But in just a few days, he was back to his normal self again, cracking jokes with me and acting like nothing had ever happened. That's just how things were with us, even if one of us was still mad. Any residual anger or resentment kind of simmered there on the surface.

I hoped he wouldn't bring it up again.

It was a Friday afternoon and we were shooting the shit, lounging around Max's basement and soaking up the A.C., when Max suggested we do something different.

"Screw this," he said. "The semester's more than halfway over, it's hot as hell, and we've done the same damn thing every day after school." And it was true, so after he and Toby bickered back and forth for a bit about whose fault that was and Connor smoked another bowl of their weed, we decided to break into the community pool.

We picked up some liquor at the Strip and drove over in Max's beat-up Chevy, relishing the quiet of the late afternoon. The pool was closed for renovation and wouldn't open until summertime, but the construction guys were gone for the day and the water was crystal clear, tempting us all, untouched by dirty patrons. The air smelled like sawdust and chlorine, and I'd forever smell that when I tasted cheap bourbon.

"Alright, fuck it, let's do this." Toby stomped out his cigarette in the grass and rolled up his sleeves.

"Hold on, man, there's like security cameras, right?" Max said.

Toby rolled his eyes. "Can you just try for once not to be a total pussy, Max?" He made a leap for the chain link fence and struggled to haul himself over as Max scrambled to help him.

Max needed some help himself to scale the fence and ended up cutting himself on the wires, but when it was my turn, I felt Connor's hands on my back, lifting me up, and the ease at which he did it surprised me. Once we were up and over I was about to say thanks, and he gestured at me to come closer, opening the pockets of his board shorts inside out to reveal a bag of pills.

"Split it with me later?" he asked quietly, when the other boys were out of earshot. I nodded, though I felt nervous.

We downed the bourbon pretty fast, blaring rap on Max's portable speakers. The water felt good even though it was pretty warm, and I floated down, testing how long I could hold my breath as the bottom of the pool spun around me.

When I came up for air, Connor was in front of me, holding out the pills. One was green and one was blue.

"Very *Matrix*," I said, but I didn't reach for one. "What is it?"

He only smiled. Shirtless in the water, I felt scrawny compared to him, even though my build was fairly average. He had an impressive set of abs, and up close, I couldn't help but notice the deep scars on his wrists that he'd never discussed. I wondered if the guys noticed them like I did.

"Alright, fine, fuck it," I said, popping back the green

one, choking a little as I tried to force it down. It was chalky and hard to swallow. "But rescue me if I drown, okay?"

Connor swallowed his easily. "You won't. But I will," then called out, "Any bourbon left, Toby?"

I'd thought I had a high tolerance, but Connor was on another level. He threw back the liquor as easily as he had the little blue pill, of what he still wouldn't tell me. I hoped it was ecstasy or some kind of upper, because the weight of the liquor was making my head feel heavy.

But things slowly got brighter, the water starting to seem more interesting, the way it rippled and splashed around my body, and I wondered how all those atoms held us together and moved so effortlessly while still remaining stable.

I tried to explain it to the boys, but by then they were out of the water, wandering around the deck trying to get better service and call some girls over.

"I'm plastered, and it's a fucking sausage fest!" Toby yelled into the empty air. Max tripped over the pool chair Connor was sitting on and started laughing even as the blood ran down his leg. Connor rolled his joint and smiled at me, and I dipped underwater and opened my eyes, enjoying the silence.

In a matter of minutes a bunch of girls came over, including Jess's girls Anna and Lizzie, wearing barely-there bikinis, massive sunglasses, and clutching bottles of Stoli. There were about six of them in all, and I stayed floating in the pool even as the boys tried to call me over, watching them gawk and drool like hungry wolves at their soft curves and breasts, the way they threw their heads back when they laughed, warm smiles glowing in the light of dusk.

"Are we gonna get arrested or something?" Anna asked, grinning and snapping her gum just like Jess did.

"That's what I said!" laughed Max.

"Babe," Toby said, wrapping an arm around Anna's waist. "The cops don't give a shit that we drink here, dope here, or that people fuckin' die in the streets in this town. You think they give a fuck about our little party here?" He snatched her sunglasses and put them on, then pummeled his chest and screamed like a wild animal while the girls cracked up, chugging the vodka straight before jumping into the pool.

It comforted me to know that Jess was home, busy cramming for some exam, far away from this drunk and horny mess.

"Where's Jess?" I heard Toby ask before I went underwater again, swimming to the deeper end, wondering how long I could hold my breath before I passed out.

When I surfaced I felt a presence behind me, and I turned to see Connor with that expectant smirk of his. I noticed how good he looked with his hair wet, water dripping from his face and down his throat. Maybe it was just the drugs talking, but I wanted to keep looking.

"Hey," I said.

"Hey."

He just kept treading water, staring at me like he wanted to say something. I felt my stomach tighten.

"So, uh, you don't want to mess with that?" I asked, motioning to the girls at the other end of the pool. "They're pretty hot."

"You think so?" he asked, splashing water across his face and slicking back his hair.

"I guess," I said. "They're alright."

"They want to fuck me," he said. It was then I noticed that his eyes were glazed over, not looking directly at anything in particular.

I laughed. "You're gone, bro."

"I am," he said. "And I feel fantastic. The pills do work their magic." He swam closer. "*They* want to fuck me. *You* want to fuck me. Everyone wants to fuck me." My stomach dropped, and I swallowed hard.

"You're cocky as hell when you're gone," I said.

"And you're a scared shitless drunk," he said.

I faked a laugh, but he wasn't smiling. "I'm not scared of anything."

He moved over to me, and I could feel his breath on my neck, smell the bourbon on it, his lips moving to my ear. "Bullshit," he whispered. "You're scared of everything.'"

Then he plunged underwater and swam away, towards the girls and the music, leaving me breathless at the edge of the water.

12

I was so restless that weekend I could barely breathe. Every time my phone made a sound of any kind, I half-expected it to be him.

Breathe, Jack. It was all I could do. Mom spent her weekend passed out in front of the TV, snoring softly with Gunther curled up at her ratty bunny-slippered feet. Dad was working at the bar. I was attempting my history essay, slogging through it in between smoke breaks and nervous glances at my phone.

Get a grip, Jack.

At around noon on Sunday my phone finally rang, and I almost jumped out of my skin. Mom mumbled something about quiet from her spot on the couch, even though the TV was blasting *Maury.*

My pulse returned to normal when I picked up and heard her voice.

"Can I come over?"

It wasn't Connor, but it was just as good.

Stepping inside my house was probably like stepping back into the 1970s, or at least what I imagined the seventies to be like from movies and TV. The wallpaper in the kitchen was old and ugly, outdated and blackened at the corners from years of cigarette smoke. The floors were cheap linoleum, the living room furniture ugly colors and patterns that clashed against the bright orange wall. We even had a zebra print rug in the dining room where Old Gunther liked to lie. It always smelled like smoke and dog and whatever woodsy potpourri Mom had put out to freshen up the air.

I hated it. It felt like living in a time warp. Jess loved it. She said it felt like home.

"Hi buddy!" she squealed. Gunther's nose went right between her legs the second I let her in.

"Hey buddy," I echoed, and I pulled her into a hug, immediately melting into her. She smelled like body lotion and sugary perfume and girl.

"Oh, it's the lovely Jessica Velez!" Mom called out from her seat at the kitchen table. She tapped her cigarette into an ashtray and smiled affectionately. "Come over here, doll. Let me read your palm."

I groaned. "Mom, do we have to do this every time?"

It was a game we'd played since I was little, some offshoot based on Grandma Selena's stories of her days as a teenage fortune teller on the boardwalk of Venice Beach, selling readings and homemade jewelry for rent money. I always wondered what it would be like to live that way, your life uncluttered, straightforward, simple. But Grandma Selena wasn't alive anymore to ask.

"Hmm, let's see," she said, pretending to frown deep in thought while she traced the lines of Jess's palm. "This line here indicates that you freely express yourself and your emotions, while this one shows you are very strong-willed."

She smirked at Jess and we tried not to laugh.

"Now the shape of your hand indicates you are perceptive, at times sympathetic, and at other times moody. Oh, but here Jess, this line is important. It looks like there will be a break, a sudden change in your life."

Jess gasped in mock surprise. "Is that bad?"

"Oh no, honey, you'll be fine. See your life is strongly controlled by fate—"

I put my hand on Mom's shoulder. "Okay, ma, I think that's enough for today."

She tossed back her hair. "You know, Jack, when I'm old and wealthy and living in a retirement community with dumb, demented, wealthy birds who think this is a legitimate science and pay me under the table to learn about their last days, you won't be invited over to my loft overlooking the city." She smirked and went back to chain smoking through her pack of Marlboros.

We went upstairs to my room. While I hated the rest of the wilting house, I loved my room—the dusty wood floors, the sloped paneled ceilings with the one skylight, and the view of the woods out back. Jess flopped down on my plaid comforter while I took out my *Ren & Stimpy* bong and lit up, taking a deep hit, the smoke curling from the side of my mouth. I love the sound of it bubbling. I offered it to her, and she took one hit before choking and coughing like she'd just tried to inhale a cigar.

"You fucker," she said between coughs. "How do you do this?"

I grinned and shrugged. "Practice makes perfect."

I had posters on the wall, autographed ones from concerts we'd been to, even one that we'd snuck into in the early hours of the morning. I remembered the smell of wet grass in the rain, mud on our sneakers, a metal bass that to us may as well have been angels singing even though we'd barely known the band.

She flipped on the TV and started up my vintage Nintendo 64 while I finished toking, letting the sweet Mary Jane fill me up to the brim with a buzzed, sated euphoria. "You're gonna get lung cancer," Jess said. "You smoke way too much."

I laughed and plopped down next to her, grabbing the other controller as we deftly moved through the motions of level one, a level we'd played many times before. It was a good talking level, something to do with your hands while you spoke.

"Other things will probably kill me before that," I said, and she elbowed me in the ribs, causing my little character to fly into a toxic puddle on-screen.

"Don't say that," she said. "Seriously, don't talk like that."

"Keep your attention on the screen, Velez," I said. "You're gonna get us both killed in a second—figuratively of course."

We finished up the next few levels in silence, the only sounds our fingers mashing against the keys and the electronic blipping and bleeping of the Mario Brothers game.

After a while we got bored and just lounged on my bed, flipping through the magazines Mom never read. I kept all of her *Cosmos*, and we laughed at the outrageous sex tips, the bizarre articles like "How to be the master of his man bits" and ways to give a hand job that sounded painful and embarrassing for everyone involved.

She lingered on the page of a busty blonde dry-humping a shirtless man, sweat dripping down his shiny photo-shopped skin. "Sometimes I wonder why I'm friends with them," she said.

I kept my eyes on the page, trying to read some secret hidden in the model's swollen watermelon boobs. "Mmm. Who? Anna and Lizzie?"

"Yeah." She rolled onto her back and stared up at the ceiling. "Sometimes I think they like each other more than they like me."

"I don't know them well enough to judge."

She nudged me with her foot. "Oh come on, Jack, you know them well enough to at least comment."

I finally closed the magazine, pushing it aside, but not before marking the page with Watermelon Boobs for later study. "They kind of…I don't know. They're not like you, Jess."

"What do you mean, not like me?"

"I don't know, you're smart," I said. "But not just book-smart, you get things. I can talk to you for three hours straight and not get bored. I don't know if I could talk to Anna and Lizzie for fifteen minutes."

"Maybe it's like you said, you just don't know them that well."

"You would know better than me, I guess."

She shrugged. "Then of course there's my mom, who suddenly wants to be all mother and daughter *Gilmore Girls* with me now that I'm moving in for a while, even though we've barely spoken since the divorce. I guess now that Kellie's in college, she needs a new plaything, you know?" I winced at the name of her sister. "A new doll to take shopping and dress up. She keeps going on and on about how my grades are so stellar I should be going to school out east, but it's like, why do *you* suddenly care?"

My phone buzzed, saving me from this conversation. It was Connor. My stomach did a somersault.

"Hang on, I got to get this," I mumbled, all awkward and sudden, ducking out of the room to catch him on the other line.

"Hey, what are you doing?" Connor asked.

"Nothing."

Smooth, Jack. Way not to sound like a loser.

And a total dick. I hoped that Jess hadn't heard me.

Why was it so easy to talk to Connor in person, but on the phone, it was like I'd forgotten half of the English language?

I licked my lips. I imagined him biting his, swirling his tongue across them, and it awakened something in my groin. I slid down to the floor in case Mom came upstairs and caught me standing there with a boner.

"So," he said, taking me by surprise, as he continually did. "What's the hardest drug you've ever done?"

I laughed nervously. "What, why?"

"Just curious. I may be looking to buy, and your tolerance level at the pool proved to be pretty solid. Thought you might want something. Toby says his cousins have good deals on certain prescription pills."

What the hell was he doing? "I told you, man, stay away from them. They're bad news."

Jess's shadow fell over me as she leaned against the doorframe, mouthing: *Who is that?* I shrugged and she nudged me with her foot.

Connor just laughed. "If you say so. But you didn't answer my first question."

I wanted to. I wanted to stay on the phone with him forever, but Jess was giving me this *look*. "Let me answer that later. I got to go."

"Oh, okay. Is your mom there or something?"

"Sort of."

After we said goodbye and Connor promised to text me that night, which sent a round of butterflies flapping furiously through my stomach, Jess just stood there and cocked her head at me, arms crossed against her chest.

"What?"

"Who *was* that?"

"No one."

She smirked. "You were talking to *no one* about doing *nothing*?"

Shit, she'd overheard me. I got up off the floor and

gave her a playful shove back into my room. "Don't sweat it, Velez. You'll always be my favorite no one to do nothing with."

I thought I saw a look of hurt flash across her face, but then she was grinning again, chucking the game controller at me. "Well, this no one can still kick your ass in *Mario Kart*."

13

Look at the woman.

After Jess left to go home for dinner—Mom had said she'd make us chili, but then just sat at the kitchen table staring at her hands for a while—I unearthed the page in the magazine with the watermelon-boobed woman and the shirtless man.

Look at the woman.

I tried to focus on the curve of her back, the pinch of a waist between her hips and chest, the long, sleek legs and manicured toenails. I felt nothing. It was like looking at an ancient artifact at a museum, an arrowhead you've seen a million times—interesting at a certain angle, but not intriguing enough to want to wrap your hands around it and feel it from the inside out.

Look at the man.

Warning bells went off in my brain. The ripped man grinned up at me from the page with his movie star teeth. His biceps. His chest. *No*. I wasn't going to fall for that. I closed the magazine and tossed it across the room.

"Act like a man," Dad always used to say. "Men don't wave like that. Wave like this. Hold your arm straight. Don't let your wrist flop like a…like a…"

He said it in the grocery store. After my soccer games. At the carpool lane at school. He never said the word itself, never finished the sentence, but I always knew what he meant. And every time I felt like I had to cry, but I couldn't. Not in front of him.

But then I thought of Connor again, of how he'd looked at me in the pool, water all over his skin. What he'd said to me. The way it made me weak just to talk to him.

This will go away, I told myself. *He's new and kind of rough around the edges and maybe a little weird, an artifact in the museum that's actually a piece of art. Something you can't quite wrap your mind around.*

14

We'd just put acid under our tongues, strips of paper printed with Scooby Doo and Donald Duck. We decided on Max's basement for the trip. It was empty and cool down there, a humming air-conditioner and stained coffee table littered with old copies of *National Geographic* and *Time.* They had some trippy pictures in that shit.

I think Toby started to feel the drugs working first. All four of us were kicking back on the couch, our kicks on the coffee table, when mid-conversation, Toby rolled up the sleeves of his Iron Maiden t-shirt and stared at his arms as if he'd never seen them before.

"Put the beer muscles away, Tobe," Connor said. He leaned back into the ratty couch, probably taking it all in for the first time: the dark oak wallpaper, the carpeting a dull gray, stained with beer and cigarette-burned holes of parties past. Max's folks never came down here. The dart board over the pool table was only touched by us now, the plastic talking rainbow bass mounted over it collecting dust on the wall, its mouth hanging open in a permanent dumb stare. The basement was our headquarters, a treehouse of sorts for rambunctious boys who were snorting something harder than Pixy Stix and no longer chucking pebbles at girls. Now we welcomed them.

Toby started humming to himself, and Max and I exchanged a smile. Toby jumped up from the couch and kissed his biceps, turning to face Connor.

"These are the real deal, my man," he said, flexing what little muscle he had.

"Yeah, I doubt that," Connor said. He shook his head and smacked his carton of cigarettes against his palm. I watched the motion, transfixed by the repetition, my head starting to feel fuzzy, all of the colors in the room giving off a warm glow.

Toby hopped from foot to foot, getting that look, that look that meant he wanted to fuck around. "You wanna try me?" he asked Connor. He put up his fists and punched the air, whistling enticingly. Max and I cackled.

"*Love* to," Connor said.

"Then come try me, you little bitch!" He looked so ridiculous, with his uncombed hair and pupils bulging, like a little boxer man in a *Looney Tunes* cartoon.

Connor got up from the couch and tossed his pack of

cigarettes to me. When the carton hit my palms, electricity surged through my fingers. It was then I knew just how high I was.

Connor stared Toby down for a moment before shoving him. Toby lost his balance and hit the ground hard, but quickly recovered, sitting up and pulling Connor down on top of him. They wrestled around, Max practically in tears from laughter, until Connor pinned Toby's hands behind his back and gave a triumphant laugh. Toby grunted and struggled, trying to break free of his hold. Max snorted and took a swig of beer, handing me the bottle to finish it off. I pressed it to my lips, realizing I was smiling like crazy, the booze tasting radiant in my mouth. The plastic bass gaped at us from the wall with his glassy, knowing eyes. I swear I saw its mouth move.

Connor punched Toby's arm once, then freed him, standing and throwing his arms up in the air. "And the *true* Iron Maiden remains triumphant!" he declared. Max whooped and clapped for him.

Toby pounced on him from behind, trying to yank him back down, but Connor easily pushed him off. Max was practically collapsing with laughter even as he ducked Toby's sucker punch. It all happened in a blur of hands and bodies and sweat, but Connor got over to me and grabbed my arm, pulling me into the dog pile.

I tried to remember seventh grade wrestling camp, tried to get Connor in a headlock like I'd learned when I was just a kid, but he was too quick. After a good scuffle—*his hands, his chest, his body*—he flipped me on my back and pinned my arms to the ground, palms pressed into mine. We were breathing hard from the exertion, my shirt up to my chin. I felt the muscles in his palms fire before they released mine and slid back to his sides. His smooth biceps, the way his tank top cinched around his taut shoulders…I forgot how to inhale. His eyes wandered down the bared skin of my chest, down my thigh. He raised an eyebrow, his lips curling into a grin.

Shit, shit. I rolled him off me and stood up quickly, adjusting my pants with fumbling fingers. My face burned red hot.

As I walked quickly to the bathroom around the corner I could feel him watching me. Max and Toby were feeling the high, I could tell from their laughs. They were—thankfully, hopefully—oblivious.

I flipped on the lights and splashed freezing water on my face, trying to breathe. I tried to visualize something soothing, tried to stop shaking.

The door opened. The lights went out.

The lock clicked.

And suddenly he was everywhere.

His chest up against mine, hands all over. The smell of his shirt, cologne that set my senses on fire. I opened my mouth, his kisses hungry and rough, nothing like a girl's. Hot tongue, hands down my back, up my shirt, blazing trails across my skin. I let it burn right through me, like the heat of the sun. I just let go.

15

The house was dead by the time I got home, save for the

porch lights Mom always left on for me. Still high from the acid, the mosquitos looked like little raindrops dripping onto my skin. I swatted them away and opened the door.

It was dark and quiet, so I kicked off my shoes and started upstairs, assuming everyone had gone to bed. I'd smoked enough weed to calm down my trip, but the staircase felt unstable and the silence was all too loud.

"Jack?"

I stopped and looked over the banister at the TV room. A lamp was on, softly illuminating the face of my father. He was reclined in his EZ chair, head slumped forward.

I walked into the room and saw them right away, about a dozen empty beer bottles scattered all over the floor. Old Gunther snored beneath his feet.

"Dad?" I asked cautiously. I was scared to move, as if one misstep would set him off into a drunken rage.

It took him a little while to look up at me. His eyes were empty and faraway, like I was merely a flicker on the TV screen. He smacked his lips and mumbled something.

I crept over slowly and kneeled down beside him. I felt five years old again, looking up at Daddy for attention, a game, or even a smile.

"Dad?"

"Your mother..." he slurred. "She's at it again. She's hiding something from me, some big plan. I can feel it."

"Can I get you something, Dad? You want some water?"

"She's been squirrely lately. Won't answer my questions directly. She thinks I'm so damn dumb. They all do. Everyone thinks old Jim's just a dummy, just a piece of white trash from a Scottsdale trailer park. But I see it all." He turned to me, eyes narrowing, pinning me to the floor.

"You hiding something from me, Jack?"

"No, sir."

He clamped his arms down on my shoulders and pulled me close to his face. His voice had gone hard and dark. "If there's something you need to tell me, something you been hiding from me, you tell me right now, you understand? Because whatever it is, I will know. I *will* find the truth."

The stench of his hot beer breath made me nauseous.

He's just drunk, he's just drunk…

"You think you're so clever, huh? Running around with your little friends like hoodlums, stirring up trouble all over town? And now you think you've got it all figured out, just picking up and going whenever you damn well please."

"Dad, I'm not—"

"You tell me right now, Jack. You tell me right now if there's something I need to know. Is there, Jack? Should I know something about you and your mom that I don't already? You two planning something?" His voice was like bullets raining down on me. His face was strained, gaze flickering back and forth across my own.

"No," I said quietly. I couldn't stop shaking.

"Nothing?"

"Nothing," I whispered.

He dug his fingers into my shoulder blades until I winced before freeing me from his grip. He nodded once, fell back into his chair, and passed out.

Now I know, I thought as I crept upstairs, retreating into the sanctuary of my bedroom. It stung, but it was better to admit it to myself now. *Now I know I can never talk to him about anything.*

16

Things went back to normal on Monday, or as normal as things could be. Dad and I didn't speak of what had happened that night, or what he'd said to me in a drunken stupor. I'd spent the rest of the weekend in my room, listening to music, smoking up the rest of my weed and even watching a few bad shows with Mom while she chain-smoked and ate peanut butter ice cream out of a tub and lied to me about all of the jobs she'd been applying to.

It was like it had never happened at all. All part of some big, bad trip down the rabbit hole.

I'd had weird dreams that weekend too, vivid and strange. It could have been the after-effects of the acid. But the dreams were tinged with anxiety. I knew partly why I'd been waking up in cold sweats from so many murky nightmares, and why the dreams grew worse as the weekend came to an end, but I tried not to think about it.

Part of me was still sure I had dreamed it.

Mom made me toast and coffee Monday morning and sat with me at the table while I ate, still shaken from the last night's sleep.

"You know, I'm thinking, if no one in this town will hire me, I might as well do what I've always wanted to do. I'll finally write that book, you know the one, right Jack?" She tapped the ashes of her cigarette right on the table. "Of course you do, I've been telling you about it since you were four years old and could barely understand me. You know you learned to read so early on, you were always such a bright little guy, full of ideas. Well I think it's genetic,

Jack, and I've got ideas of my own. I've got a lot of stories to tell, stories your father hasn't even heard, stories that'll have the big shots in New York banging down my door for a finished manuscript..."

She sipped her morning screwdriver and spoke mostly to herself, bouncing around ideas in her head that seemed to fluctuate without rhyme or reason. I nodded passively, my leg jiggling under the table, half-anticipating a text or a call as an excuse to get away from her.

I biked to school by myself, not bothering to ask Max or Toby to join me or give me a ride. I needed to feel the quiet around me. I sat outside under the shade of an oak tree in the courtyard before the morning bell, watching kids laugh and talk and smoke. It all seemed so exhausting, all of the energy that went into every conversation, every turn of the head, every gesture and expression.

My mind wandered back to Dad.

His own dad, my Grandpa Jack, was a Gulf War vet who flew an F-14 Tomcat during Desert Storm, spraying the caked earth with missiles. Shrapnel was still lodged in the crevice of his elbow, right up until he died. As a kid, I'd sit on his back porch on hot summer nights, Grandpa Jack telling me stories about Vietnam and World War II by the light of the fireflies. I cupped the little bugs in my hand and pretended to listen, holding them gently in the cocoon of my palms. They felt so safe there, the way their tiny legs tickled my skin as I silently told them I loved them.

I knew Dad would never understand something like that. He liked to trap them in mason jars for hours. They would suffocate in their glass prison as their mini-engines leaked their chemical lifeblood until they shriveled and died. I'd cry and Dad would always tell me to stop being a pussy about some goddamned bugs in a cup.

That summer I turned eight, I played outside, scraping my knees and collecting insect specimens for study. After dinner, when everyone was settling down for the night, I'd go out and lay in the grass, watching the stars. Back then they seemed to burn so big and bright in the black sky.

I like to tell myself I went out there almost every night because it soothed me, because outside the air was clean and free of cigarette smoke and the stars intoxicated my budding imagination. I'd pretend those memories were clean and pure, just a little boy's fascination with the galaxy outside his warm California home, while inside Daddy smoked his pipe and watched the evening news and Mama knit by the fireside.

I used to lay out there in the cool lawn, letting the universe roll over me and swallow me whole, pretending that I didn't hear the television blaring and the sound of my daddy's garbled words underneath like static, the sharp pops of aluminum cans opening and the clanking of bottles in the fridge. The expanse of sky would drown out my mother's screaming, her lungs scratched raw from ash and tar, our TV turned up so loud the whole house shivered. Things being broken over and over again.

One evening I just up and ran away. It was around the time Dad lost his job, the big one at the company two hours north of town. That one that bought us fancy dinners at the steakhouse and weeks of Mom acting close to happy. I was young, but even I understood: those days were gone.

I slipped through the fence and headed up the street, watching the insides of people's houses, the glow of domestic tranquility playing out behind painted shutters and flowered curtains. The air smelled like evening barbecues and the eucalyptus trees that dotted the sidewalks. As I got closer to the Strip, the lush green lawns faded to brown, the concrete littered with cigarette butts. I passed late-night bottle shops and express markets with their big fluorescent signs, teenagers huddled at street corners smoking and shrieking with drunken laughter. A bum spat on the street and kicked pieces of broken asphalt at the sides of parked cars, muttering to himself. He scared me.

I was getting tired and my feet hurt. I wondered if my parents were worried, if I should have left a note or something. But then I remembered I was running away and picked up the pace. I couldn't give up now. I ended up in front of Grandpa Jack's apartment building and hit the buzzer.

"Hello? Who—who the hell's out there? What you want?"

"It's me, Grandpa."

"Who? Who is this?"

"Grandpa, it's me. Jack."

I could hear him wheezing over the intercom, some sports game on in the background. "Jack? Is that you?"

"Yes, Grandpa."

"Well, what the hell are you doing out there? Do you know what time it is?"

"Grandpa, can I please come in?"

"Does your father know you're here?"

"No."

A pause.

"He with you?"

"Nope."

A few moments passed, then the door gave a sharp buzz and I went inside to the smell of mold and cats. Someone was playing the radio too loud down the hall, the noise bouncing through the paper-thin walls like a boomerang.

Grandpa was in his old checkered bathrobe, his wrinkled face unshaven. He shook his head and let me in.

Inside, the TV was blaring and it smelled like mold and pipe smoke, a comforting and familiar scent. I took a seat in his EZ boy and propped my feet up, watching the poker game.

He turned off the TV and took a seat across from me, lighting his big, funny pipe. We sat like that for a while, me getting sleepy in that big comfy chair, him puffing away. We didn't say anything. Nothing needed to be said.

Our silence was broken by the ringing of his landline. He'd never quite figured out how to use a cell phone.

Grandpa got up to answer it, and I closed my eyes tight and clenched my fists, praying it wasn't who I thought it was.

"Yeah…yeah, Jim he's with me. Don't you worry. Huh? What was that? Oh, I invited him over. I told him to visit me tonight…in my letter!…well, how you would know that, you don't read his damn mail! Uh-huh. Mmhm."

I imagined Mom pacing in the kitchen, screeching questions at my father about where I was, what had happened. My stomach did a somersault.

"Oh, well okay…I know, you had a long day, Jim, I hear ya…mhm. Maybe you should think about heading off to bed, hmm? No, I didn't see that one, I was watching the poker game. Alright, well I'll tell him. You tell Ellie to calm herself down, alright?"

He hung up and turned to me, studying me carefully. "You just stay here tonight, alright Jack?"

Early the next morning he drove me home, but didn't even walk me to the door. I knew he wouldn't go in with me, even though I had hoped with all my might he would, and when we reached my driveway he just gave me a sad little shrug and a smile and said "You know how your daddy is," before driving off.

I felt my teeth chattering as I softly knocked on the front door. No answer. I waited a while before trying the knob and found the door was unlocked. Inside, it was dead silent, not even a peep from our noisy puppy in his crate. Then I noticed the mess.

Shreds of paper were scattered all over the living room floor. Mom's favorite lamp was sideways on the ground, the beautiful lavender globe cracked open. As I passed the kitchen, I spotted the broken bottles and something shiny and red on the cheap linoleum. I took a few steps over, feeling hot and shaky. There was broken glass and a trail of dried blood.

I tiptoed upstairs and climbed into bed, the blue-tinted darkness of the cloudy morning pouring through my blinds.

I lay awake, unable to sleep for what felt like hours. Then I flinched at the creaking sound of my door opening, but in a moment, there was only the sound of it closing softly.

When I woke up, the house was empty of my parents, the living room now eerily pristine and tidy, as if last night had never happened. Our puppy had been let out and was lying on the sofa, wagging his tail at the sight of me. I found a packed lunch on the table—Mom's work, no doubt—and a note in Dad's jerky handwriting: "You can walk yourself to school from now on." They'd left without me.

I took the lunch bag and our puppy Gunther and headed down to the creek a few blocks away, a little forgotten stream that fed into the storm drains. I folded up the contents of the lunch bag and skipped them across the water, letting Gunther lick the wetness from my face.

17

Connor texted me during Spanish, right around the time Mrs. Banks started droning on about verb conjugations. The difference between *I have, I had.* What the fuck did it matter, anyway?

Willow Park on 3rd after school?

Not the usual half-assed jumble of acronyms the boys sent me. I wrote back quickly, holding the phone down between my legs so Banks couldn't see.

Sure.

I checked to make sure I was in the clear. The last thing I needed right now was to get my phone confiscated. Thankfully, Banks was busy scrawling something across the board, starting up her daily speech on the importance of bilingualism in the U.S.

"English may be our first language, but that doesn't make it the most important. It's important not only to recognize but to *celebrate* diversity in this country. I mean, whether or not the conservatives like it, we minorities *do* exist." That got a chuckle from about half the class.

I waited for the familiar buzz of my sound-dampened cell.

"Besides," she said. "It would be boring if only one kind of person existed. More than one type of person makes life more interesting, gives us more to appreciate. You guys following me?"

A vibration in my lap like a jolt made me jump. I pressed unlock to read my phone and then the air felt denser, harder to breathe.

I miss you already.

The park was nearly empty when I got there, save for a few kids laughing and chasing each other across the jungle gym. Their parents leaned back on the benches, reading their books and finishing work assignments on their laptops, enjoying the nanosecond of freedom from parenting in the warmth of the sun.

I spotted Connor under the big, gnarled oak that provided a welcomed canopy of shade. He leaned against the trunk, looking up at the sky, a small smile resting on his lips.

I felt a tingling in my belly and tried to breathe, taking a seat next to him in the grass, stretching out my legs. He wore his favorite black board shorts, a fitted white tee hugging his chest.

"Hey," I said. I sat there cross-legged, pulling at blades of cool grass nervously. My stomach wouldn't settle.

He inhaled deeply. "You ever think about the atmosphere, all of those clouds, and all of it up past there? The stratosphere, the mesosphere, all the way up to the iotosphere and beyond into space…"

"You mean the ionosphere?" I asked, uprooting another blade of grass.

Connor finally turned to look at me. "Well, shit, look at the brains on you, Jack." He laughed and tugged at my shirt, using it to pull himself up. I couldn't help but stare, my gaze wandering down to his cheekbones, down the square of his jaw, to the bare skin of his collarbone barely visible…

He pressed his lips to my ear. "Do you want to kiss me?"

I shivered and nodded, unable to speak. Somewhere not so far away a little girl screamed and a mother started yelling, probably at her. I could almost feel the eyes of the other parents on us under this tree, some magnetic pull sparked by a protective urge to shield their young from anything unwanted lurking on the edge of the park.

"What's wrong?" he asked. His lips grazed my throat and I gasped.

It took some hidden strength of will to pull away from him. I turned away from his pressing stare, watched a mother push her daughter on the swings. The little girl kicked her pink shoes into the air and squealed with delight. "*Higher, Mommy! Higher!*"

"I can't," I murmured at the ground. "I just can't. I'm sorry."

"You had no trouble with it the other night," he said, but the playfulness in his voice was strained.

"It's the park, all these people," I said, fishing for some way out, some easy explanation. How could I explain it? How could I even begin? "I just…I can't in front of them."

Connor laughed and I finally turned to look at him

and his upturned grin. He pushed back his shaggy black hair. "Alright, man, come with me."

He stood up and thrust his hands in his pockets. I just sat there and looked up at him.

"Don't worry, I'm not going to do anything. Scout's honor. Just come with me." He nodded in the other direction, away from the park. I stood and followed him.

We walked for a while in silence, the air cooling to a breeze. We went down a neighborhood street filled with holes in the pavement, past boarded-up houses and a billboard advertising bail bonds. We met the main roadway and turned a sharp right, flanked by speeding cars trailed by heavy exhaust fumes and a shopping center, chain stores, and pizza shops huddled together in their cement enclave. No sounds but the rush of road noise. Connor finally turned and started heading down a steep sloped hill of overgrown wild grass, a small forest meeting it at the bottom.

It was easier to just gun it down the hill, or so I thought it'd be. I tripped once but he grabbed my arm before I hit the ground. We finally made it to the trees. It was shady and cool in the forest, a little stream ahead that we jumped across.

"Where the hell are you taking me?" I finally asked, breaking our unspoken pact of silence.

He grabbed my hand and pulled me into a sunny clearing, a little grove encircled by forest, not a house or car or road in sight.

"I like to come here when I need a second to myself," he said, pulling me down next to him. "Some guys deal here at night, but until sunset we're solid. It's beautifully quiet, isn't it?"

And it was. All you could hear were the birds chirping in the treetops, the sounds of the freeway muffled to a distant, faint roar.

Connor pulled out a pack of cigarettes, smacked them against his palm and offered me one. We sat there smoking, soaking up the sunshine.

"So, talk to me, man."

I shrugged and stared at my sneakers. "What about?"

"What are you so scared of?"

"What do you mean?"

He laid back in the grass and took a deep drag. "You know what I mean." His voice was thick with smoke, sounding just like Mom's after she'd filled her lungs and sinuses. "Of me. Of how you feel. It terrifies you."

I bit the inside of my lip. "I'm not scared, just... confused."

He frowned at me, eyebrows raised. "About what? That you like boys?"

My face grew hot. "I'm not a fag or anything if that's what you're thinking."

He put his hands up in mock-surrender. "Hey, I didn't call it that, *you* did. I don't mind labels myself; I'm bisexual. But, whatever. I see the way you look at me, like the way chicks do when I'm out at the skate park with my shirt off and I've got sweat running down my back."

The image made me feel hot all over. "You look at *me* like that," I said defensively.

"Yes, I do. Because I like you."

I said nothing, and started yanking up fistfuls of grass

and tossing them aside. My chest felt tight, like the way it did for years in church when the preacher started going on about sin and loose living, the bonds of marriage and all that horseshit. Parenthood, the way we were made, the way we were intended to be by His Holy Highness who lived up in the sky, take a left at the ionosphere. The way my father sat attentively during those sermons in that hot chapel that smelled like old lady's perfume, his eyes glued to the preacher in reverence, fat mouth open slightly, breathing loud, hot and wet. And he forced me to come every single Sunday until I turned thirteen, when I would throw the biggest tantrums imaginable, screaming and stomping my feet until they gave up and left me at home.

"Is it your friends? They don't know shit, Jack," Connor said. "They're just as insecure as the rest of us."

In my mind, there was Mom in her Sunday dress from Walmart, that cheap piece of shit in puke yellow that smelled like mothballs, staring blankly at the floor.

"You're amazing, Jack. I know you don't see it, but I do."

"Don't call me that," I said. "Girls say that shit to each other." I pulled the cigarette from his mouth, took a drag, and stamped out the butt in the grass. It tasted like our kitchen.

"Maybe girls have the right idea. We could learn a thing or two from them, you know."

I remembered being in my starched dress shirt tucked into the only slacks I owned. I kept my hands in my lap, wishing I could be anywhere but there as the preacher went on and on about how homosexuality desecrated the sanctity of marriage and would be the ruin of our society. My palms were sweaty, my throat felt itchy, and it was like everyone in the congregation knew my shameful secret.

Fuck the shame.

I kissed Connor hard, pushing him deep into the earth with my lips. He slid his hand under my shirt, up my back, opening his mouth to welcome my tongue.

18

"Hey Connor."

We were standing by the lockers, just hanging out in between periods, when Skye Russo and her posse appeared behind us. All doe-eyed and glossy-lipped, Skye stood there lingering in front of Connor, her friends close behind, pretending to be oblivious but wearing knowing smiles.

Connor turned away from me and smiled at her, leaning against the locker. "Hey, what's up?"

"Um, we…"

Her friend stepped in. "Skye wanted to invite you to our party this weekend. Her parents are out of town, and you know the drill."

"Lots of uh, refreshments and fun times," Skye said with a waggle of her eyebrows, and her friend gave her a look. "Sorry. I mean there is, but…you should come."

"Yeah, okay. Give me your number," Connor said. He reached for his phone but Skye grabbed his hand and pulled out a pen, writing it on his hand. Her friends laughed. "See you in psychology, Connor."

He turned back to me. To whatever was on my face. "What?"

I shrugged. "Nothing. Have fun at your party."

"You should come with me," he said, inching dangerously close. "We can do…all kinds of things."

I took a step back. "Yeah, maybe."

"What's wrong?"

"Come with me," I said, pulling him into the nearest bathroom. I pushed open all the stalls, checking for people.

"We can't do that…in front of people, Connor."

He frowned. "Do what?"

"You know. You can't act like that around me here."

"Oh right," he said, rolling his eyes. "You're scared someone will see—your friends, what they'll think of you. God, fuck it, Jack, we should go to that party and go out in a blaze of glory! Just show up like it's no big deal, I mean what are they gonna do if they—"

"Connor," I interrupted. "How long have you gone to this school?"

He frowned. "Long enough to know that this place is royally fucked up."

"Yeah well, it is fucked up and it's worse than you think. I just can't do that, okay? Not here. Not right now."

He sighed and nodded. "I got you. I used to be like that too, before I stopped giving a shit about what other people think. But I get it. Trust me, I do." He took my hand. His skin on mine was like flipping a switch on my mood. "You should come with me to the party."

"Why?" I said. "There'll be plenty of hot girls like Skye there."

"I don't care," he said.

"I thought you liked girls."

"I do." He leaned in and kissed me. "But I like you more."

I felt myself smile.

"Anyway, you have to come. They have a hot tub. Big fancy house. Or at least that's what I heard Skye bragging about to her friends in Spanish."

"Shut up."

"No, I'm serious." The bell rang. "I'll see you at lunch, okay?" He kissed my cheek and left the bathroom just as a group of guys came in, startling me out of my daze.

I spent the next period doing what I usually did after Connor kissed me in between classes: nothing. I couldn't concentrate, could barely think. Buzzed and high, like I was full of helium.

The rest of the week was clouded by him. He was what I saw when I closed my eyes, and it sent my stomach into knots, my chest full of fire. His voice, his laugh, the way he put his hands through his hair, it was mesmerizing. I watched the way he breathed, fascinated by each intake of air and each exhale, the way his stomach rose and fell. The way his face looked when he was relaxed.

He was addictive in other ways too. He brought me some of the best weed I'd ever tried, better than the shit Toby's family sold. We toked up that beautiful Thursday right after school let out. He brought a glass pipe decorated with peace signs and the most amazing stuff I'd ever inhaled.

Things were going beautifully when Jess's voice broke through my stoned half-consciousness.

"Jack? What the fuck are you doing?"

She stood there, arms folded, scowling at us like she

was part of the security team. Bad students, no smoking on school grounds.

Connor leaned back in the grass and started laughing hysterically. We both had the hoods of our sweatshirts pulled so tightly over our heads you could barely see our faces. I walked over cautiously, looking around for security. Half of me didn't give a shit. It was such a great afternoon, the blue sky, the THC swimming through my blood, Connor's elbow so close to mine it gave me goosebumps.

"You guys want to get kicked out of school?" she hissed.

"That's why we're in disguise," Connor whispered, pulling the drawstrings tighter until I could barely see him.

"Hey, Jess!" I said, waving the pipe around. I wanted her to let loose and relax, crawl inside the moment with me. "You gotta try this shit. I swear, you will not—hey!"

She snatched it out of my hand before I could finish another sentence. "Are you serious? Go home and smoke this, dummy. Why are you sitting out here in the middle of the courtyard smoking up in *broad daylight*?"

I was too stoned to form a coherent response, so I grabbed it out of her hands and sat back down on the soft grass. I took a long hit. "It's cool, Jess. Everything's cool. The grass is green and the sky is blue."

"Jack, please, I'm serious. Can you just walk me home?" She rubbed her bare arms like she was cold and it wasn't so hot I was baking to a crisp inside my sweatshirt.

"Seriously, dude," Connor said, nudging him in the shoulder. "She's serious, man. Like, seriously." Then we were both cracking up all over again, two ridiculous cartoon character boys.

"It's not funny, Jack!" I heard the desperation in her

voice, but somehow felt so far from it. "Can you just come over here for a second?"

"Yeah, yeah, give me a minute," I said. The pipe was full of sweet stuff. Just one more hit…

"Jesus, forget it! You're high as a blimp." She turned and started to walk away. "I'll leave you to your new *best friend.*"

"Jess, wait! I didn't mean it!"

"You are such an asshole, man," I heard Connor say, and again, in spite of the fact that I had just been a massive jerk to my best friend in the whole world, we broke into laughter. I watched her leave, arms folded tight across her body, head down, and felt a pang of sudden guilt, like the feeling I got as a kid when I'd snatched these balloons from a little girl on the playground and let them float away into the air, higher and higher, both of us faced with the sudden realization that they were gone forever and all we could do was watch them leave.

19

"Did you know that a whale ejaculates like 100,000 gallons of sperm a day?" Max asked us.

Toby laughed so hard you could see the yellowed molars in the back of his mouth. I stubbed my cigarette out in the grass.

"Gross," I said. It was lunch period and we were sitting in the green, far enough away from the courtyard they wouldn't see us covertly smoking some nice hash Toby had scored for us that morning.

"And get this," Max continued, flipping through his phone. "Ducks have like, the largest penis in the world. They're like fucking explosive springs. Look at this, man."

Toby grabbed his phone from him. "Jack, look at this, look! It's like a fucking rape pole!"

I moved my head away. "I don't want to see that."

"Speaking of which," Toby said. "We should go fishing tonight."

Max's eyes lit up. "Yes! At Skye's thing!"

Toby groaned in appreciation at the mention of Skye. Gross. "Forget the fishing. We'll go just to see what slutty ensemble Skye picks out tonight."

"I don't know if I feel like it," I said.

He gave me a look. "You never fucking *feel like it*."

"Jack, are you kidding? It'll be dope," Max said. "We haven't gone to a legit house party in forever."

I scoffed. "Forever" was barely more than a month to these losers. I looked longingly across the green out to the courtyard, wondering where Connor was. Lately I'd been feeling less and less connected to my boys, like they had shrunk into tiny gnats that wouldn't stop biting at my skin.

And as for "fishing," well, that was Toby's favorite evening activity, a game that involved picking up girls. It had its own set of rules, and like the sport, they weren't always so nice. The idea was to nab the ugliest girl there, the so-called "fish," and then compare them all at the end of the night after they were all too high or drunk—or both—to notice.

It was Friday and expected that it'd be really warm tonight, so plenty of girls would be wearing tight, tiny outfits to Skye's party. Toby and Max were still talking about the beached whales they'd find there when I stood up.

"Where you going?" Max asked.

"I'll be back."

I knew Toby was watching me as I walked over to the courtyard, closer to the shade.

I checked for security and lit a cigarette. From my spot beneath a beech tree, I could see all of the kids sitting and eating on the grass, laughing, talking, probably joking about the latest thing they saw or did online, some shit like that. I saw the nerdy kids huddled around in a circle playing that Magic card game—playing with intensity, the kinds of kids that Toby would laugh at. They noticed when he did that shit, but I never said anything to him.

I scanned the red brick building of the school, the stucco walls and the ugly puke green doors, the ones I passed through every day. I wondered what it would be like to get lost in that sea of faces, really lost, like as a new kid without a past and without an identity…without any friends or baggage of any kind.

"Hey man."

I turned and saw Max, smiling sheepishly at me. "Toby said to come see what you were doing. You okay?"

I shrugged. "Why wouldn't I be? I'm fine."

"I don't know. You just seem…kind of distant lately. Like something's bothering you."

I laughed dryly. "Thanks, but I really don't need a therapist. I'm just chilling. Alright? I'll meet you guys later."

"Yeah, about that," Max said, turning once to look over at Toby. "You really should come to Skye Russo's crib tonight. It's gonna be sick, like mad chicks and drugs. We just talked about it and we've decided we're meeting here."

He pulled out a pen from his pocket and took my hand

in his, turning my palm upwards. For a moment, I felt a cold dread go through my stomach, but it fell away as soon as he started writing down a time and an address.

"In case your phone goes dead or something," he grinned. "Or in case you forget."

There was Max's sweet, unassuming smile. I opened my mouth to say something. There was something I wanted, *needed* to say to him, though what I couldn't quite figure out.

20

Toby and Asha Yardley were grinding to some shitty rap song.

The beat dropped, and his arms were around her waist, her ass pressing into his crotch, my head dizzy from the wine coolers.

The place reeked of bad weed, ash, and tar, but the energy was electric, the air on fire with the pulse of noise and sweat and bodies. It was manic in here, in Skye Russo's basement, the lights dimmed to a cool blue.

Toby and Asha were grinding, and there was me on the sidelines, sitting on a leather couch, smoking the complimentary weed that was probably laced with something bad. Whatever it was, I was already starting to feel it. Whether it was the weed or the wine coolers, the room was fuzzy around the edges, everything moving fluidly before slowing down and then starting right up again to the sound of the bass, like we were trapped inside some trippy music video.

Asha was all skin in short-shorts and a barely there top. Good girl Asha, student government Asha, her breasts—breasts usually hidden beneath crisp polos and denim blouses—heaving over her low-cut shirt.

Max was right next to them as Toby's hands gripped her neck, her eyes closed, pressing her body against his. The weed was making my mouth taste funny and sour. Max, with his own girl for the night—or the last few minutes of this song—was in heaven, wearing his sunglasses like a douche. Some guy sat down next to me and spilled beer on my shoes. Toby was beckoning me with his head, his hands preoccupied with the edges of Asha's shorts.

I turned away and tried to pretend I hadn't seen, but I had. His hands had lingered there for a moment before climbing up inside.

I stood and pushed past the mass of bodies, sticky and warm and shouting, until I found the door and climbed upstairs into a lighter form of madness. Kids were tipsy and stumbling around the kitchen, playing poker and beer pong on tables that were covered in plastic just for the occasion. They were making out in every corner, spilling drinks all over each other in this gorgeous mansion.

It was seriously a beautiful house, at least for Burro Hills. It reminded me of those Spanish colonials I'd seen in Mom's magazines, with high-beamed ceilings, stone floors, and spacious living and dining rooms with ornate rugs and drapes that probably cost more than most people's rent in this town. It was the biggest piece of property in Burro Hills, save for the old abandoned movie theater on the Strip that used to show spaghetti Westerns. Skye's parents spent most of their time away on business, leaving Skye blissfully unattended. She was the richest kid we all knew, and naturally, her home was host to many parties. Rich, and she always got her way. Her parents had wanted to send her to some prep school in the Bay Area or out east, but she'd refused. For some reason, she loved it here. Probably loved being the richest kid in town, loved how good her grades looked compared to ours. And rumor had it she had an army of private tutors at her disposal. We usually didn't go here, the guys and I. It was the kind of place football assholes would flock to, but it was a nice night for a trek up to Skye's tiny, gated community right on the cusp of our school district. Plus, we were out of weed, and Toby's cousins were using his basement.

I was surprised to hear Jess would be there that night. Skye Russo had made her life hell freshman year, slowly and carefully eradicating her from their clique. Now dozens of drunk high school idiots—and probably some local community college kids too—were turning her house into one whacked-out frat party. I spilled some of my beer on one of Skye's expensive Persian rugs, watching the dark ale stain the fancy fabric. Karma is a bitch, you know?

Then I saw him. The music seemed to evaporate from the room, and everything inside me went still and quiet. Connor and Skye were pressed up against one another, grinding against the wall. Her eyes were closed and her head was tilted back. She leaned against his chest, and he kept his hands on her waist.

I turned and pushed through a throng of people, suddenly needing fresh air. Guys cursed at me as I knocked into them and shoved them aside, until finally I'd found my way out onto the terrace, where a group of kids were taking shots and smoking under the silver light of the moon.

My phone beeped. I ignored it, lighting a cigarette to quiet the rumbling in my chest that felt like someone was pounding on it, slamming fists into my lungs. I tried to breathe, but my phone kept on beeping incessantly.

A text from Jess and a text from Toby.

Jess's read: *Leaving now, see you soon! :) Get me a drink!*

And Toby's: *Come back downstairs. Mad hotties down here. You'll love 'em.*

21

I was sitting so close to the speakers that I could barely hear my own thoughts. I occupied the leather couch facing the center of the room, where I could sit and stare vacantly at the crowd and no one would bother me or try to ask me my name. I was on my fifth jungle juice and on my way to going completely numb.

Connor and Skye Russo. Skye Russo and Connor. The walls around me were beginning to swim.

Toby appeared with a shot in hand. He was wearing Max's beanie. I took the shot, letting it burn my insides, then snatched the beanie off his head.

"What the fuck?" he said.

"Doesn't suit you," I said. I tossed it at a drunk girl nearby, some college-looking girl with long legs and a low-cut dress. She swayed to the music, smiling as her eyes went in two directions. She giggled drunkenly, pulling it over Toby's eyes and leaning into him.

I toasted my empty shot glass in his direction, then went back to downing my jungle juice. Not five minutes later and he was back, leaning close to me so I could hear him and smell the liquor on his breath, that awful smell that reminded me of my father.

"Which one do you want?" he slurred at me, nodding to the room full of girls.

I shrugged. "None. I'm good right here."

He laughed and shook his head. "Jack, dude, it's been like thirty minutes. Don't be shy, I can hook you up with any of these girls right here. I swear. Swear to God. They won't turn you down as long as I'm doing the talking."

He was drunk, super drunk, and I wanted to tell him to get the fuck out of my face and mind his own damn business. But I just leaned back, took another sip of juice and shrugged.

"Her," I said. I was just pointing at random, but I realized with relief that the girl in my finger's direction was none other than Jess herself.

I watched Toby's smile vanish for a moment. And then his grin was back, and he was laughing to himself, but his eyes hadn't changed.

"I thought she was like your *sister*," he said. "I thought she was off the table."

"What's that?" I said. "Speak up, Toby, I can't hear you."

"I said…I thought…" He leaned in closer to me, almost stumbling on the slippery, sticky floor. "I thought you know, maybe if you don't want it, I could hit that."

He must have taken my scowl to mean he'd made me

jealous or something, because he put his hands up and shook his head. "Nah, she's all yours, Jack. I get it. I don't get why you're so weird about it, but it's cool. You should go for it. You shouldn't wait. Don't be a little bitch about it."

I stood and moved to leave the room, but not before bumping shoulders with him and murmuring, "You would know about being a little bitch."

22

I couldn't believe it was Jess. I had never seen her like this before.

She was plastered. I could see that even from here. She must have pre-gamed with her friends. But what was scaring me was how old she looked in that tiny little black dress and those high-heeled boots with spikes all down the heel, how old and young at the same time. She wore thick make-up, and her long, platinum hair tumbled down her shoulders in waves. From across the room, she smiled and waved at me, wobbling in those silly boots. She put a hand on the shoulder of some guy to steady herself. His eyes were up her dress and he was grinning like those creepy old guys at Bazingo did when a pretty girl walked into the room. My throat tightened.

It was all Toby and Max had been able to talk about, this Jess who had just stepped out of a magazine, or off the runway, or out of the screen of some trashy Hollywood reality show. They were looking at her like she was their next meal.

"So, you gonna do it?" Max asked, nudging me in the ribs.

"Just fucking do it, Jack. Look at her." Toby whistled appreciatively and took a swig from his cup.

They'd been goading me for what felt like hours. Time was beginning to blur. The room could swallow me whole in one gulp. I shook my head to try and steady my vision.

I watched her swinging her hair back and forth in time to the music, her dress riding up her thighs, revealing hot pink underwear.

"You little bitch, are you nervous or something?" Toby laughed. He was joking, but it didn't sound like a joke. "I mean look at that. *Damn.*"

Words were stuck in my throat. I swallowed them down.

"Nah man it's fine, listen," Max said, leaning in close to slur in my ear. "It's easier when they're drunk."

He must have learned that from Toby. Or had I said that to him at one point? Why would dweeby Max say something like that? My brain tried feebly to piece it all together, to make sense of the tilting room and the noise penetrating my brain. Everything felt like a dream, like I was swimming through light and sound that was all inside my head. But in that surrealistic moment anything felt possible.

Toby nudged me. "Hey, if you don't want her Jack, I do." I looked him in the eye, and that coldness was still there, that steely look that made me feel sicker than all the liquor I'd just downed.

"Uh, hello? Jack, do you need another drink for courage or something?" Max asked. Someone bumped into me and spilled booze on us, and Toby shoved them.

"Asshole!" he yelled. "These sloppy kids. No one knows how to hold their liquor anymore."

"Yeah," I said, watching Jess shake her hips to the pulsing beat.

Look at the woman.

Max started to say something else, but I pulled away and began moving over to her. She was swinging her hips so hard she nearly tripped. I grabbed her arm.

"Oh shit, thanks, Jack!" she said. Her face was red and flushed, her eyes watery and a little faraway. I led her over to the leather couch in the center and helped her into it. She slumped onto my shoulder, letting her arms fall across my chest. From the other end of the room, Toby made a dick-sucking gesture with his mouth. Max was laughing, his Adam's apple bobbing to the beat. I turned away.

Jess was breathing heavy. "You okay?" I asked her.

She nodded, lifted her face up, and looked at me through her hair.

"Mm, yeah," she said groggily, resting her head on my shoulder. "Everything's super cool."

I watched her belly move up and down as she breathed, studied the way the light hit her face and curved down her lips. I tried to imagine touching her, what it would feel like, how it would be. A little part of me tried to hold back, but I pushed it aside, letting the drunkenness fully take over, and leaned in to kiss her softly on the cheek.

My lips lingered there for a moment. Her skin was surprisingly soft.

She blinked at me sleepily, all doe-eyed and gentle, and yes, she was pretty, and maybe this time I could feel something. I leaned in closer, pressing my lips to the corner of hers and letting my hand rest on her shoulder blade. Then she jerked away suddenly, like I'd done something wrong.

I could feel Toby watching me, could see him moving closer in my peripheral. Why couldn't she just cooperate, for one second? Play drunk and oblivious like she had with that guy she'd let feel her up a second ago? What was so wrong about me?

I stroked her cheek with my finger and ran my hand down the small of her back to her exposed bare leg, feeling the soft skin and the warmth of her body. She mumbled, "Jack, what are you doing?"

"This," I whispered in her ear. I pulled her towards me and kissed her. She froze for a moment. My hand crawled up her thigh. I'd hooked up with girls before, more or less, but I'd never touched them. I'd always just let them touch me. Would it burn my fingers, would it hurt? Strange thoughts circled my head, but they somehow made sense. I touched her under her dress and she gasped, then grabbed my wrist and pulled my hand away like I'd tried to bite her.

With our faces so close, I could see her eyes were dark and bewildered. "What the fuck are you doing?"

"What's wrong?" I asked, and then it was like a light had been flipped on and I could see again. A hot wave rolled over me from head to toe, and I knew then that I could never take this back.

"What's *wrong*?" she mocked, recoiling from me. "What the hell's wrong with *you*?"

It was like being socked in the stomach. "Me? There's nothing wrong with me. You were all over that other guy just a second ago. What, am I not *worthy* enough, Jess, to touch your body? I know you know how many guys have been staring at your ass in that tiny dress all night. You haven't exactly been telling *them* to fuck off."

The slap landed harder than I'd expected. It took a moment for me to register the pain across my face, I was so numb with drunkenness. She got up from the couch and stormed off, and I didn't go after her. I just sat there, feeling the shame and anger burning right through me. I punched the couch and pushed through the mass of bodies that now felt suffocating, refusing to make eye contact with Toby and Max. I just wanted to crawl into a hole somewhere and never come out.

I spotted Toby follow Jess down the long hallway. I knew he was going after her, but I didn't move to stop him.

23

I didn't deserve to get out of bed. I deserved to lay there all day, my stomach pitching, my head pounding like someone was banging a steel drum inside of my skull.

At around noon, Mom crept into my room and pushed back my hair, feeling my forehead. She came back a little while later with hot soup, and when I moaned and rolled over, refusing to touch it, she just patted my back and left it on my nightstand.

I didn't stir until my phone buzzed hours later. A text from Connor, asking if I wanted to meet downtown.

I sat up too fast and the whole room tilted forward. I sprinted to the bathroom, trying desperately to puke up the bile I could feel inside of me, but nothing came out, not even when I stuck my fingers down my throat. So I splashed my face with cold water, brushed my teeth, gulped down three aspirin and gelled my hair as best as I could. I still looked like shit. My eyes were hollowed out, my face bloated and puffy from the alcohol. Fantastic.

My stomach growled from hunger, but the soup was too cold to eat by then.

I deserved it all. After leaving Jess in the lion's den of the party, I had drunkenly biked the four miles home to my house, bearing all the cuts and scrapes and bruises on my legs to prove it. Then I'd stumbled upstairs and taken the coldest shower of my life, trying to numb everything. My skin wouldn't stop burning.

By the time I made it downstairs that afternoon, Mom was at the table doing a crossword puzzle, wearing her signature bathrobe. The TV was on, and I was surprised to see Dad plopped in front of it, lounging in his La-Z-Boy with Gunther curled up by his feet. My faithful dog snored loudly.

"Dad, don't you have work today?" I asked.

Mom coughed and muttered something about the puzzle she was doing. "He's sick too, baby."

Right in front of him on the TV tray was a bowl of the same soup Mom had made for me.

"Well, look who's finally up," Dad said. He spun in his chair to face me, and we locked eyes for a moment. Father and son, two hungover, useless bastards. If someone had wanted to paint a portrait of our family lineage, this would've been a good place to start. "What are your plans for today, Mr. Mysterious?"

"*Heaven only knows*," Mom sang from her spot at the

table. "You don't look so well, Jack. Maybe you should go back upstairs and get some more rest. I could bring you up a crossword puzzle. They've got some good ones today."

"Thanks Mom, I'm fine," I mumbled, and I hurried out the door.

"Mr. Mysterious," said Dad.

I took the bus to the Strip where Connor said he'd meet me. It wasn't too crowded since it was a Sunday—a lazy, humid Sunday, people in shorts and flip-flops, the bus blasting AC so cold I thought I might freeze to death. I watched beat-up cars drive by, cars with two different colored doors. Homeless men and women wandered up and down the streets. At a red light, I watched a woman so big and heavy she could barely waddle out of Goodwill pushing a shopping cart stuffed with baby supplies. She had three screaming kids trailing after her, and an infant strapped to her chest. Her face was tomato red, and she was sweating and panting from the exertion. A knot formed in my throat.

I don't know why, but I wanted to reach out and take her hand and lead her away from here, guide her to a place that didn't smell like burning pavement and gasoline and exhaust fumes. Maybe somewhere by the ocean with a cool, balmy breeze. I wanted to make sure her kids got presents every Christmas, nice ones that lit up and made cool sounds, presents all the other kids would be jealous of. Not presents from the Goodwill that were probably broken and smelled like mothballs.

But by the time the bus coughed me up and I saw Connor, leaning against the old movie theater, smoking a joint, I forgot how to breathe, how to think straight. I forgot about the waddling woman and her kids and my parents and the homeless people on the sidewalk.

I shuffled up to him, hands in my pockets, wishing I hadn't worn jeans on such a hot day. He was cool as a cucumber in cargo shorts and a t-shirt that gripped at his biceps.

"Finally," he said when he saw me. "I waited as long as I could to light up."

I checked over my shoulder for cops, but all I could see was a woman with dreadlocks sitting on the curb with her pit bull, holding up a cardboard sign that read: *Hungry and pregnant.* I wanted to toss her a quarter, but Connor was watching me, and his pull was too magnetic to resist.

"How are you feeling?" he asked. He took a long drag on the joint, then handed it to me.

"Like shit," I said. "You?"

"Not too bad," he said. "Of course, I didn't drink nearly as much as you did. I didn't even know it was possible for a human being to drink that much."

He was grinning, but I turned away.

"Sorry, did I say something wrong?"

I shook my head.

"Are you still pissed about that girl at the party, Skye, or whatever her name is?"

I must have looked surprised, because he laughed. "I saw you eyeballing us from across the room. I swear, we didn't do anything."

"Yeah, whatever, man." As soon as the marijuana filled my lungs, a calm rush took over my body. I handed it back to him.

"You don't believe me? I had to do something while you were downstairs chasing after chicks."

I snorted. "That was them, not me."

He took a long drag and held out the joint, but when I reached for it, he pulled it away. "Then how come all I've heard these past twelve hours is how Jessica Velez is now in with Skye Russo's group because they all think you tried to force your tongue down her throat last night?"

I coughed so hard I thought my lungs might burst open. "What? What are you talking about?"

He shrugged. "Word travels fast. Apparently, they feel so bad for her that they've taken her under their wing, whatever that means."

Skye and Jess had been good friends in middle school. But the summer before high school, Jess went to visit family in Colombia. She came back confused about the rules and the convoluted new social hierarchy of Burro Hills High. She would cry to me every day while I tried my best to listen. There would always be a new fumble she'd made; the humiliating mistake of wearing a sparkly Hello Kitty backpack, singing Disney songs to herself in the halls, or raising her hand too often in class. It made me dizzy to hear it all. How did girls come up with these rules? Soon the whispers started, just low enough so the teachers wouldn't pick up on it, but loud enough so that Jess could hear. I wanted to stop it, but there wasn't anything I could do. I didn't understand why these girls who'd once been her closest friends were now treating her like the enemy. Notes were passed, rumors started about her being a secret slut, even sluttier than Kellie. Girls would trip her in the halls, girls that used to braid her hair and make her friendship bracelets. Someone even slammed her into a locker once and ran away laughing. Skye orchestrated it all, the puppet master behind the scenes. I even confronted her at one point, asking her why she was such a bitch, but that made the girls even madder at me, and they punished Jess even harder. So I kept quiet, stayed in my lane.

But Jess was a warrior. She never let them see her falter, keeping her face stoic at school, holding her head high in the hallway just like I'd encouraged her to. She ate lunch with me and the guys, pretending it didn't bother her that even the most unpopular of girls wouldn't go near her. But after school, after we'd make it back to my house and the safety of my room, she'd collapse into tears and bury her head into my pillows, letting out animal screams. It wasn't until she met these new girls, Anna and Lizzie and their wind-up bimbo friends, that she started to smile again.

After all of that, all that she'd been through, how could I have treated her like I had? I not only didn't deserve to get out of bed and see the sunlight and stand here and smoke with the most beautiful guy I'd ever seen, I didn't deserve to breathe.

I stared at Connor, a very beautiful, very cocky new kid, this kid who hadn't even been here for a full four months and suddenly had all the intel. "How do you know all of this? How do you even know these people?"

He just shrugged. "What happened between you and Jess?"

"Nothing happened. Hand me that."

He held it out of reach, then finished it off and stomped the roach out on the pavement. "Bullshit, something always happens or no one would say anything. Especially not with Jess. Isn't she like, your best friend?"

I watched the homeless woman—or was she a vagabond?—accept a dollar from a homeless man from across the street. A businessman yapping into his phone passed her by without a second glance. "I…I don't know. I was really drunk, and Toby and Max wouldn't shut up, and I don't know why I did that. I don't even know who I was in that moment."

"That's very existential of you, Jack," Connor said. He sidled up closer to me. "It's alright. You guys just need to talk it out. And anyway, it was a really terrible party."

I said nothing.

"Look," he said. "It wasn't cool what you did to Jess, but you should talk to her, clear things up. Tell her about Toby and Max and why you were acting like such a dick that night." He leaned in, and I could smell his cologne, feel the heat of his body. The steel drumming in my head moved down to my chest. "Now can we just go back to being friends or *bros* or whatever?" His fingers were on my neck, a danger zone.

"Knock it off," I said, pushing his hand away, fighting a smile. "We're in public."

"We don't have a very captive audience, if you haven't noticed."

It was true. Aside from the vagabond woman and the homeless man, there was only the occasional pedestrian absorbed in their own lives.

And he smelled too good, way too good. It should be illegal to smell that good.

"What are you thinking about?" he asked.

"How you smell," I answered, way too honestly. *Nice, Jack.* "I mean, your cologne. It smells nice."

"*You* smell nice," he countered. Now his fingers were in my hair. *Shit.* He was practically purring in my ear. "You always smell nice." *Mayday.*

He tasted like peppermint and pot when his lips touched mine. The world around me dissolved for a moment, and I all I could taste was his mouth, but then I remembered kissing Jess and had to pull away.

I was pond scum. I was lower than pond scum.

But Connor didn't seem to mind, let alone notice. My stomach growled so loudly I thought passersby might hear it.

"Want to go get lunch?"

I shrugged. "Can't. I'm broke."

"I'm buying," he said. "Seeing as though I deprived you of those last few hits of pot, I figure I owe you."

"Okay. I just have one question." I inhaled him again as he leaned in closer to hear it. "What the hell does *existential* mean?"

24

"Is security outside?"

"Nope, we're good."

"Then let's go," I said.

We drove off-campus in the middle of the day, something that could get you suspended at Burro Hills High, but we needed our fast-food runs. The best lunch deals were always at White Crest Plaza, just a mile up the road. Usually it was just one of us who went and grabbed food for everyone—it was safer that way, less risk of getting caught—but it was so nice out that morning that we all decided to just fuck it and go as a group. Connor was doing his pay-for-tutoring thing that period and raking in some mad cash for almost no work on his part. He'd hired some bored brainiac kids to secure test answers beforehand and sell them out. Connor was like the Don of the group; you had to visit him, pay upfront, and then your answers would be distributed to you at a designated time and place.

"See, I don't give them *all* the right answers, at least not their first time. That would make it too obvious," Connor had explained to us that morning before school. "Teachers would get suspicious. Things would go under really quick. You give 'em like seventy to eighty percent correct, and suddenly kids who are flunking Algebra are doing fairly well, little by little, and who do they thank? Me. Me and the guys in the tutoring room while we get paid under the table."

"That's fucking awesome, man!" Max had said.

"But what if they snitched?" Toby asked. He rolled his eyes in my direction.

"Why would they?" Connor asked.

"Maybe they feel ripped off. Maybe they think fifteen dollars a test isn't good enough. Maybe they threaten to crack the system unless you lower your price."

Connor's smile curved at the corner of his mouth. "You don't get it, Toby. These kids aren't that smart. They're desperate. This is their first taste of power and control.

Why would they ruin it? And if they did, they'd be outcast, blackballed. No one would talk to them. It's foolproof."

"Whatever, man."

It was a pretty sneaky, well-executed operation, and one of the coolest things someone had ever pulled off at our school. And it had kept him busy all semester.

Now it was just me and the guys grabbing some food, and after listening to lectures all day, I was ready for some much-needed peace and quiet in my day.

"Whoa, whoa, look at that!" Max said as we pulled into the parking lot. He pointed to my neck.

No such luck.

"Damn, Jack," Toby said.

"What?" I said, my hand instinctively going to my throat.

"Is that a hickey?"

"Oh shit, that's huge," Toby said, stomping out his cigarette and looking closely. I flinched and moved away from him, my face growing warm.

"Come on Jack, don't be shy. Let us see!" Max said.

"Who's that from?" Toby asked.

"Did Jess give that to you?"

"Shut up," I said, walking ahead of them. "You guys are such perverts."

"*We're* the perverts? She was pretty upset the other night," said Max.

"Yeah, what did you do to her, man?" Toby asked. "If I had Jess, I'd treat her real nice. *Real* nice, you feel me?" I heard Max laugh.

"I said *shut the fuck up*," I said. They went silent, as if stunned by my tone and the way I'd said it. I didn't care; I just wanted them to leave me alone.

We got our food and drove back to campus, Max and Toby ignoring me the whole way back. I felt restless, and all I wanted to do was get the fuck away from them, away from everyone.

So when the bell rang, I snuck outside and grabbed my bike, making sure security wasn't on the lookout for assholes like me. I biked up the street, down into my neighborhood, past my house where Mom was probably inside watching trash TV, down past the strip mall where Dad was working the day shift at the local bar, and then onto San Juan Boulevard, where the creeps and addicts were out.

I parked and locked my bike next to Bazingo, which was strange to see in broad daylight, with no shining marquee lights or long line at the front. Inside, with its depressing black floors and black walls, I found Toby's uncle who owned the club. He sold me something that I snorted in the bathroom stall. It helped ease the anxiety gnawing away at my insides and quieted the thoughts racing each other in my head.

Once I was high enough, I stepped outside into the cool night and sat against the side of the nightclub. I'd finally gotten the courage to dial Jess's number. She'd been ignoring all my texts and calls, all my repetitions of "hey" and "I'm sorry about the other night." She'd been ghosting me, and I knew she was ghosting me, because I could see whenever she was online.

The phone rang and rang, and I kept on redialing until she finally answered.

"What do you want?"

I rubbed at my eyes. I could feel a splitting headache coming on. "Hey Jess. Listen, I know you're mad, and I'm really, really sorry. About the party. About what I did. And—"

"What exactly *did* you do?" she asked sharply.

"I…well, you know. I kind of, accidentally came onto you, and—"

"*And?* And what, Jack? Listen, I don't want to talk to you right now. I don't want to see you. I mean, I can't risk having you *accidentally* slide your hands up my skirt again."

A car swerved by and splashed dirty water on me. I deserved that.

"What was that about, anyway?" she asked. "Do you like me or something? Because that's a really fucked up way to show it."

"I…"

"All those years we were friends," she went on, and I could hear, the way she was holding back tears. Shit. "All those times you came over, hung out with me in my bed. Were you just waiting to make a move on me?"

"No! Jess, I don't like you like that," I said. "I just—"

She laughed like it was the dumbest thing I'd ever said to her. "Oh, so you're not even *attracted* to me? You just wanted someone easy to hook up with that night? Is that it? That is so impossibly pathetic."

"Listen, please. Toby was goading me all night, he wouldn't shut up, and I was really drunk and—"

She scoffed. "Oh, so now it's *Toby's* fault? Are you fucking serious, Jack? You know, he actually came to comfort me afterwards. I was a crying, drunken mess in Skye

Russo's basement bathroom, and unlike you, *he* came to see if I was alright."

I'll bet he did, I wanted to say.

"Jess, please just let me—"

"I really can't deal with you right now," she said, cutting me off. "Don't call me. Don't text me. Just leave it, Jack. I need some time."

Now it was me that felt like crying.

"Okay," was all I could say before she hung up, the dial tone painful in my ear.

25

The doorbell rang, and we could see him through the window.

"You didn't tell me your friend was Mexican," Dad said.

Jesus Christ.

"Or handsome, at that," said Mom.

"You're both disgusting," I said.

I opened the door to Connor, all bright-eyed in a fitted navy blue tank top, thin gray cardigan, and his signature board shorts. His hair was slicked back in a way that looked purposeful yet effortless. "Hey," he said to me. I studied the way his lips formed the word.

Dad shook hands with him, squeezing a little too hard around the knuckles. "Nice to meet you."

Mom continued the weirdness, extending her hand like some twentieth-century debutante. "Pleased to make your acquaintance."

Connor took her hand and kissed it gently, playing along with ease. "The pleasure's all mine, Madame." Mom practically swooned, giggling and attempting to light her next cigarette seductively. I had to look away; I just couldn't deal with it. It was like something out of a bad movie.

"Alright, my room's this way, and—"

"Now hang on a minute, Jack." Dad put a hand on my shoulder. "You hungry, Connor?"

"Dad, I don't think he's—"

"Um, sure, what do you got?" Connor said. He turned and grinned at me over his shoulder before following Dad into the kitchen.

"Mom." I stretched the word into a groan.

"What?"

"Don't *do* that."

She waved her cigarette around dramatically. "Do *what*?"

"You know, act weird…around my friends."

"Well it's not every day you bring a hot little number home." She smirked.

"Okay, now I'm definitely going upstairs."

"You like chili, Connor? We got some nice black beans here too somewhere…"

"Alright, Dad," I said, coming into the kitchen. "You've been a very gracious host. Connor, let's go to my room."

"Nice to meet you!" Connor called out as I practically dragged him out.

Upstairs in my room he sprawled out on my bed, put his arms behind his head, and grinned up at me.

"Your dad thinks I'm Mexican."

I closed the door and locked it. "I know. He's a racist asshole. They're super weird, and I apologize on their behalf. But uh, what are you, anyway? If you don't mind me asking."

"Chilean, as far as I know. Maybe a little bit of Colombian too. And no...I don't mind you asking. You can ask me anything."

I sat down beside him.

"Jess is too," I said.

"Huh?"

"Jess is Colombian too. At least, I think she is."

"Think? Isn't she your best friend?" he asked, tossing a pillow at me.

I tossed it back, thinking back to the awful conversation from last night when I was high out of my mind. "I honestly don't know anymore."

"You want to talk about it?"

"Not particularly," I said. I reached for my bong.

"Fair enough. So um...*vous avez du feu*?" he said.

"What?"

"I said, can I get a light?" He pulled a cigarette from his pack.

"You know French?"

"Enough to borrow a lighter," Connor grinned, sticking the cigarette behind his ear. He sat up and edged closer to me on the bed. "And enough to maybe try to impress you, a little."

I tried to conceive a universe where Connor Orellana had to try to impress *me*.

He shrugged off the cardigan. His lips on my neck broke my next thoughts, dissolving them like mist until my head was empty and open and all I felt was him. He reached out and tenderly stroked down my cheek, trailing his finger across the bone. Something just below his hand caught my attention.

"What's this?" I asked, gently touching a deep scar on his wrist. He pulled his arm away quickly, like I'd burned him.

"Nothing," he said, shaking his head and moving his mouth to mine. "Just an accident."

I let him unbutton my shirt and slide it off me. I shivered as he kissed up my chest to my throat, flicking his tongue against my ear. I felt wired and restless, an awkward puppet without control of its own strings.

"Are you nervous?" he whispered.

"What?" I said. "For what?"

He laughed a little at the tenseness in my voice. "Nothing," he said, kissing me. "Just relax. Unless…you want me to stop."

"No, please don't," I said, feeling unsure. "I just…I can't. Not here." I nodded at the door.

"Then let's go," he said.

"Where?"

"My place. Don't worry, no one's home."

I must have seemed anxious, because he followed it with: "And don't worry, I'm not going to tie you up and skin you alive in my basement or anything. Not unless you want me to, that is."

I laughed and buttoned my shirt, grabbed my keys and followed him out the door. All the way to the bus stop I felt like flying.

Up in his room, with its high wooden ceilings, multiple skylights, and clean white sheets, I felt less edgy, less like I always did when I was at my house. Connor poured me a shot of Fireball whiskey and we said "Cheers" and drank it back, me enjoying that sweet cinnamon burn down my throat. His room was so cool, so modern, with shiny wood floorboards, a white shag rug and a poster of a young, hot Marlon Brando next to one of Jourdan Dunn. He had a lava lamp on his dresser, a keyboard and a guitar propped up against his floor-to-ceiling windows, and one of the sweetest desktop computers I'd ever seen.

"Damn, are you loaded?" I asked, slipping out of my shoes and plopping myself down on his bed. It was comfortable as hell.

He laughed and turned on his computer, playing a mix of country and ambient music. "Nah, but my uncle is. And he's very generous."

He slipped out of his t-shirt and tossed it aside, and I felt myself harden at the sight of his bare chest. He took off his jeans, revealing black briefs that hugged his ass just right, and it was then I realized how hard I'd been staring.

"It's okay, Jack," he said. He sidled up to me and joined me on the bed, rubbing my shoulder. "Just relax."

I'd been having dreams about him like this for nights, but seeing him here in person…it was paralyzing. "I'm just…I'm…I'm sorry, fuck, I'm—"

"You're nervous," he said gently. He pressed his lips to my shoulder and looked up at me. "Look, you don't have to do anything you don't want to do. No pressure."

"Can we drink a little more first…before we…"

"If you want, but I don't want you to be hammered for this. If you do want to have sex, I want you to be relaxed, comfortable, and present."

Sex. Fuck. The virgin inside me was terrified, and a

part of me felt ashamed. Ashamed I was a virgin, ashamed of how scared this was making me…but mostly, secretly and awfully, ashamed that I wanted to have sex with him. I wasn't exactly sure what that would even entail, or how it would feel, although the thought undeniably turned me on. I'd seen some gay porn before, curiously browsed through it…but in porn it was all so animalistic, so hard, and even painful.

"Have you ever…had sex with a guy before?" I asked him.

He nodded.

"And did you…how do you…"

He kissed my cheek and started stroking my hair. "I can show you. I'd be gentle, I'd go slow. But only if it's what you want."

I thought for a moment. "It is what I want."

I was nervous and scared and felt a little awkward, but Connor made everything easy. He seemed so experienced, and damn, he was so sensual. We peeled off the rest of our clothes and laid down on his bed, and he spent time kissing every inch of my body, my shoulders, my neck, my stomach, down between my thighs, until finally he started blowing me.

I'd tried letting a girl do this to me before, but *this* was a whole other universe. With the girl, it had been uncomfortable and unsexy, but with Connor…damn, it was incredible. Then he kissed me deeply, introduced me to the wonders of lubricant and the importance of condoms, and when he went inside me it hurt at first, but soon began to feel like someone was hitting the most amazing sweet spot that I'd never known I had. And the whole time he was asking me things like, "Are you okay?" and "Does this feel good?" and it did; it felt so, so right.

I lost my virginity to a Johnny Cash song, and afterwards, Connor lay on top of me, our breathing heavy, his warm skin against my bare chest, feeling euphoric and calm and maybe even a little emotional.

I also felt something growing inside me, an affectionate warmth for Connor that I'd never felt for anyone before. We untangled ourselves and just lay there, shoulder to shoulder, basking in the glow. Just for that moment, all of the fear I'd been holding onto evaporated.

26

Max was shaken that morning, more so than he usually was. He and Toby were lingering in the courtyard, speaking in low voices, looking over their shoulders every few minutes. All around them people were talking about something, their lips and eyes moving so fast I could barely make anything out. Something had happened, something big. A security guard had one sweaty hand on his belt and the other clamped around a walkie-talkie, muttering into it every few minutes.

Connor and I had ridden to school together, something I'd feared would cause unwanted attention, but no one seemed to notice when we parked and locked our bikes side by side. No one said a word or seemed to see when Connor's hand brushed mine, or when he turned to give me a smile that set off a thousand fireworks in my stomach.

I was being paranoid. I was sure I was. Connor and I were speaking in Morse code, an undetected language. To the casual onlooker, we were nothing more than good friends.

But then we approached the guys, and Max dropped a bomb.

Riley Adams had been found by a janitor early in the morning next to the auditorium, lying unconscious in a pool of his own blood. His glasses were broken, shattered around his face. Someone had snapped a photo before security found him, before the ambulance was called. And the photo was circulating fast.

Max showed it to me. I could have puked right there. Riley had been stripped naked, his body covered in Sharpie drawings of penises. I shook my head and pushed it out of my sight.

"Who's Riley?" Connor asked. "Why would anyone do that to him?"

Toby grunted. Max looked down at his feet.

"He's a theater kid," I said softly. "Really…uh, really outgoing."

We had an assembly about it before first period, an assembly that lasted nearly an hour. Principal Oliver stood on stage, looking grave and ashen, promising us that whoever did this would not only be caught, but held responsible. Connor and I sat next to each other. We'd managed to lose Toby and Max in the shuffle of nervous bodies, and in the darkness of the auditorium, under the seat, he squeezed my fingers.

The guys behind us kept laughing, muffled snickers and comments made under their breath. Ten minutes in,

Connor turned around and said, "Could you please shut the fuck up?"

They stared at him like he was off his rocker, as did I. These were the Rudoy brothers, Jerry and Mike. They were friends of Toby, so by extension—even though I hated those football meatheads—they were friends with me.

"You got a problem, man?" Jerry asked. He leaned in closer to Connor, a lion ready to pounce. A lion with a very low IQ and the best tackle on the football team.

"It's cool," I said, pinching Connor's arm to get him to turn back around. But he was staring them down with this look of disgust I didn't know he was capable of. It was starting to freak me out. "Don't worry about it."

But Connor—this idiot—he didn't budge. "Some kid got the shit kicked out of him, and you assholes think this is funny? Have some fucking respect."

"Respect?" Mike said. He was just as big as his brother, and almost as ugly. "Let me tell you about respect. Maybe he deserved it. Maybe he didn't show respect, and he needed a lesson in keeping his little hands to himself."

Connor's nostrils flared. Onstage, a guidance counselor was talking about tolerance and safe spaces in our school, *blah blah blah*. Was she as dumb as the Rudoy brothers? I pinched Connor harder, but he pushed my hand away.

"Are you saying you did that to Riley?" Connor asked. "Are you actually dumb enough to be incriminating yourselves right now?"

I could tell neither of them knew what incriminating meant, but Jerry spoke up for his brother.

"No, no, we're just saying," he said, slapping his brother on the back. A teacher walked past us and shushed us with such ferocity I thought it might stop them, but it didn't. "We're just saying that we've heard things."

"Gentlemen!" the teacher snapped.

"Yeah," Jerry said, looking directly at Connor. "So, you should probably shut your mouth and not start rumors, motherfucker."

"That's it," the teacher said, snapping her fingers at Jerry and Mike. "Get up, both of you. We're going down to the principal's office since you two clearly can't keep your mouths shut for five seconds."

They freaked. Jerry pointed at us and said we were talking too. Mike looked like he was ready to spit on us. I was sort of surprised he didn't.

"Come on! Hurry up!" the teacher said. I'd seen her around before, some new teacher, fresh out of grad school. She wore pantsuits and heels every day, like she had something to prove. She didn't understand this place.

And she clearly wasn't ready when Mike lost his mind and yelled, "The principal's *onstage* right now, you dumb bitch!"

Everyone in the auditorium turned to stare, even the principal and the guidance counselor, who seemed particularly scandalized. She was new here too. The teacher's face went so red I thought she might combust on the spot.

I thought Connor might be gloating, or nervous or something. But he was just sitting face-forward in his seat, his face contorted with anger, digging his fingernails into his palms so hard a droplet of blood formed on his skin. I reached out and gently pulled his hand away.

Security swooped in and forced the Rudoy brothers up and out of the auditorium, which was now abuzz with excitement—kids with their phones out, taking videos, chatting excitedly. Onstage, Principal Oliver took off his glasses and rubbed his face.

In my mind, I could see the fear in Riley's eyes when they pushed him up against the wall and punched him, knocking him out. I could hear the crunch of his glasses breaking, taste the blood, smell the floor cleaner, and the Sharpies, and the sweat.

I wished I had been there. To protect him, somehow. To stop them.

But if I had been there, if I had seen it happen, what would I have really done?

27

Things have a strange way of blowing over, especially at Burro Hills High. By the next week there was another scandal, a major fight between two members of two rival gangs, and most everything about Riley Adams was swept under the rug. Riley either transferred schools or dropped out to be homeschooled. No one was sure. Whoever had attacked him had been meticulous, as there were no fingerprints found, at least according to Max's extensive research on the crime scene. He became obsessed with the story like some deranged private investigator, tracking every local and national news outlet for a scrap of information. Toby thought the whole thing was stupid. Connor refused to talk about it, which was fine by me. I wanted to bury it into the farthest recesses of my brain.

The Rudoy brothers were suspended, so we didn't have to worry about them for a while. I had a feeling Toby would talk to them, make things cool down. After all, they bought their pot and the best 'roids money could buy from his family.

I spotted Jess a few times with Skye Russo's crew. They all wore heavy eyeliner, blow-dried their hair into Hollywood perfect waves, and painted their nails matching pastel colors. I missed her like hell, but she seemed so happy and giggly with them. I figured she'd been happier with them than she could ever be with some asshole like me.

Besides, outside of school, I had found my nirvana.

I cuddled into Connor's shoulder, wrapping the strewn sheets and comforter around us. All I could hear was the hum of the air conditioner and his heartbeat. We stared up at the high-beamed wooden ceilings of his room, light oak panels flanked by skylights. Fading sunlight poured down on us, casting beams that stretched out across the sheets and our bodies.

"You smell so good," he murmured into my ear. "Don't stop using that aftershave."

I laughed. "It's from the dollar store."

"Save those pennies, then," he said, and I smacked his arm.

I traced the scars along his wrist with my finger, across the dip and groove of a faded cigarette burn, down the path of one lone vertical line that moved dangerously along the surface of a vein. I wanted to kiss down that wrist, every cut and bruise and burn. After we'd had sex for the second time, he'd told me the truth about them. How he'd self-harmed whenever he was angry, or scared, or sad, or lost in a sea of depression. When he thought too much about his parents or they didn't return the letters that he wrote to them in prison.

How he'd stopped now. He said he was done. I really hoped he was done.

"Can I ask you something?"

"Ask me anything."

"How did you do all this?" I asked. "Didn't it hurt?"

He was quiet for a moment. "I didn't really feel it at the time. It was…it was a way of relieving all the emotional pain, you know? All that pent-up shit inside of me."

"But were you trying to…?"

"Kill myself?"

I swallowed the lump building in my throat and nodded.

"Not those times," he said quietly.

Feeling like I'd entered an uncomfortable zone, I switched gears. "Have you…ever been with a girl?"

"A couple times, yeah."

"What was it like?"

"I mean, I enjoyed myself, if that's what you're asking." He grinned. "I like girls too, remember?"

I watched the steady rotation of the fan, the way the light and shadows were chopped and split by its blades.

"Jack?"

I turned to Connor, who was staring at me funny.

"You good?"

"Yeah, yeah. I'm fine." But I wasn't so sure it was true.

"Have *you* ever been with a girl?"

I tried to think back to all the girls I'd kissed—at parties, at dances, on the bus, on "dates." Girls with soft lips that crushed into mine, their long lashes and gentle hands. Dry-humping in basements and bedrooms while the girl moaned and moved in my arms while I groped around blindly trying to feel something.

I remembered taking freshman Jade Torrence to Homecoming my sophomore year, hugging her waist and keeping a smile frozen on my face while we stood in our tuxes and dresses as the parents took picture after picture of our group. She was chill and funny as hell, and we had a great night, leaving the stupid dance in the gym—where everyone was grinding to heavily censored music—to go smoke pot in the woods and drink. After a lot of vodka, she tried to kiss me, shoving her tongue between my teeth and reaching for my crotch, but I stopped her and took her home, held her bubblegum pink hair while she threw up on the sidewalk. When her friends found out about my "heroic deed," they started flirting with me in the hallway at school, and I humored them because they were young and silly and freshmen.

And then, there was Kellie Velez…but no, I would never go there.

"No," I answered. "Not really."

I remembered seeing porn for the first time at ten years old, in a friend's basement with a group of boys. We watched a video of a busty blonde going at it with a vibrator, her mouth open and pouty like the lips of a doll. All the boys watched boggle-eyed and laughed and cracked jokes and said things like "Nice!" and "Yeah, that's it, baby!" and I said those things too because I thought that's what you were supposed to do. But the whole time I kept staring at her eyes that looked so empty, like something sad was buried inside her.

"Jack, it doesn't matter."

Connor's lips interrupted my memories, and they slipped away as his kisses grew deeper and our bodies pressed into each other and moved as steadily and rhythmically as the beating of the fan above us.

28

I had no desire to see the guys that day, so I didn't go to the lockers in the morning. I took a quieter route out of the building and was almost in the clear, but right in the parking lot they caught up with me.

"Hey, man!" Max called out. Toby was trailing behind him, hands deep in the pockets of his dark-washed jeans. They stood in front of me, expectant, waiting for me to be my usual self, but I wasn't feeling like that lately.

"Hey," I said, nodding and forcing a smile. The only thing on my mind was getting to Connor's place, being with him in that private, secret space where I could finally take off the mask and let myself just *be.*

"You coming tonight?" Toby asked.

"To what?"

"Uh, the BMX race, man. Remember?" Max asked. "It's tonight on Pine Street."

"There's gonna be an assload of hot girls there," Toby said. He smirked.

"Oh, *right*," I said, feigning disappointment. "Shit. I can't. I've got plans with Connor."

Toby and Max both frowned. "You guys are always doing stuff together," Toby said, but it sounded more like a question than a statement.

"What are you guys, like, secretly fucking?" Max joked.

I forced a laugh. "You're sick. We're going to this thing his uncle's throwing."

"What thing?" Max asked. I wanted to hit him.

"Um, just this art show thing," I said. I started walking away and they followed me, still waiting for something.

"Art show?" Toby asked, the tone in his voice shifting.

"Yeah, it's like an exhibition or whatever. There's probably going to be free drinks there, so..." I shrugged.

"Yeah, listen man," Toby said. "We've been meaning to talk to you about that."

My heart hit a road bump, and I stopped walking. "About what?"

"Well, I mean, Connor's cool and all, don't get me wrong. But...there's something about him. Something off. And well, he's kind of..." He let the sentence trail off purposefully, waiting for me to fill in the blank.

"Kind of what?" I asked. I thought I knew what he was getting at, but I didn't want to find out. "He's chill. He's down for anything. Isn't that like us?"

"Well, I don't know," Toby said. He squeezed my arm a little too hard before releasing it, then stared me down like he was studying me, trying to see through some gap in my façade. Or was he? "Connor's definitely chill, sure, but he's a little...?"

"He's a little what? What, you mean...*weird?*" I snorted.

"Well yeah, kind of," Toby said. "Now that you mention it."

"How is he weird?" I asked, a little too defensively. *Chill out, Jack.*

"I mean, think about it, Jack," Max said. "He's secretive. He's always doing his own stuff, always kind of in the background until something crazy goes down. He got into it with the Rudoy brothers at the assembly. I mean, who's dumb enough to do that? There's just something odd about that guy."

Toby leaned in close to me again, giving my shoulder a pat. Something in his big brown eyes flashed a warning before softening again. "We're just looking out for you."

Even I had to laugh at that. "You guys are such assholes."

But Toby was serious. "Just think about it, Jack."

"Listen, I'd love to stay and discuss this thrilling topic of kind-ofs and maybes…but I got to head out. Alright?"

We said goodbye, and I unlocked my bike and rode the hell out of there, tasting relief in the air. But once I'd pedaled far enough down the road, a thought popped into my head.

What if they knew?

No, they couldn't. How could they know? They were just jealous, jealous and pissed I wasn't spending so much time with them anymore. But those thoughts didn't calm my mounting anxiety as I rode down familiar streets, letting the spring breeze fill me up with smells of freshly cut grass and blossoming trees, trying to calm my nerves. I took some deep breaths, pushed it all to the back of my mind and finally parked in front of Connor's place.

Lately it was the only place that I felt safe. I wondered how long that would last.

29

I knew it was a bad idea right when Toby spotted them.

It was the next day at school. Max and Toby had dropped the Connor thing, for now at least, and decided to let him eat with us at lunch. The courtyard smelled sweet from the budding eucalyptus trees. We were sitting there, the four of us, just hanging out and eating sandwiches, sunglasses on, when Lizzie and Jess strolled by in their tight high-waisted shorts, Lizzie in dip-dye orange and Jess a matching dip-dye pink.

Jess looked stunning. Her long, blonde hair was pinned back, revealing a face full of make-up, expertly done. She was like a girl out of a magazine, red lips and Betty Boop eyelashes. I tried to smile at her, but she just pressed her painted lips together and nodded once.

Toby, of course, couldn't resist.

"Hello ladies!" he whistled, waving them over. He lifted his shades and Lizzie lifted hers in greeting, giving him a toothy grin. "What's up?"

Jess trailed behind, one hand awkwardly gripping her arm. I could tell she really didn't want to be here, and it hurt a little. They sat down in the grass beside us.

"Smoke?" Max asked, taking out a cig for Lizzie.

I opened my mouth to say something about potentially getting caught, but decided against it. Toby had already started smoking, his gaze trailing over the curve of Jess's thighs as she sat with her legs folded on top of each other, letting Toby light her up.

"It's so nice out!" Lizzie said, tossing back her super curly hair. She had new extensions in every other week. This time they were the color of cherry cough syrup.

"Very nice," Toby agreed, putting his sunglasses back on to hide his sleazy gaze.

We sat there for a little while, chatting about mostly nothing. I'd been tuning out for a while, trying not to look at Jess while she tried not to look at me, nodding along to whatever someone said, watching people pass by us. My heart was thumping so hard that I started to sweat. I wanted to reach out to her, talk to her again, at least let her hear me out. *I'm sorry I'm sorry I'm sorry* was all I could think.

Then I heard Connor break his usually observatory silence. He always did that, waited and watched for a while until he caught a moment to say something good, something that would catch you off guard.

"No, you do *not* want to live in the fifties, Liz."

"Why not?" Lizzie asked. "I think it would be awesome. Back then, girls didn't have to work; we could just hang out and smoke and go to the beach. We didn't have to go to college and everything. Like I know, obviously we're supposed to think that's important now, but I don't see what's so wrong about wanting to live an easy life. No bills to worry about, no pressure to be some huge success."

"You romanticize that shit," Connor countered. "You think you want to go back and live then, but trust me, you really don't."

Lizzie frowned, the freckles on her nose forming a crinkly pool. She looked over to Jess for support.

Jess just shrugged. "I think the old dresses are pretty."

"Yeah, like vintage," Lizzie gushed.

Connor rolled his neck around and leaned forward, ready to lay in on them, but Toby cut in before he could speak.

"Actually, I think I'd like to live in the fifties too," he said.

"Really?" asked Lizzie.

"Really?" Jess asked, her voice thick with disbelief.

"Really," he said. "Think about it. Muscle cars, open roads, pin-up girls. That shit was great. Who doesn't love all that?"

Lizzie nodded. "Things were less complicated back then, I feel."

"You're both way off," Connor said, though he had a way of saying things so smoothly that it never sounded like an insult. "It wasn't a good time at all."

"How do you know?" Lizzie teased, blowing a ring of smoke at his face. "For all you know, it was way better than now."

There was a moment of awkward silence, and I could feel Connor bristle beside me. We all watched and waited for him to speak.

"You know, Lizzie, you say that, but you're a woman, and women had almost no rights back then. They were getting beaten by their asshole husbands who were traumatized from the war. That was just on the cusp of the civil rights movement, when black people would get lynched and people like me were considered illegals even when they fought along white men in the trenches in their white man's war. McCarthyism, race riots, police brutality. Are you kidding me? You have this candy-coated ideal of how the world was but do you know the first thing about the Los Angeles riots, which by the way, didn't happen all that far from here? Segregation in the military?"

Damn, he was so smart. How did he know all of this stuff? I was about to ask more questions, but Toby laughed darkly, cutting me off. "Oh Connor, our history buff." He patted him on the back. "This kid's a riot."

"I'm not joking," Connor said.

Toby shrugged. "Whatever man, things suck now too. And if you ask me, a lot of those Mexicans deserve to be deported, stealing our jobs and shit. I mean, talk about bad times, our town getting clogged up with all kinds of illegals from south of the border, fucking crackheads and wife beaters too. No offense to you, man."

I winced. Connor held Toby's gaze for just a moment, his voice thick with venom as he said: "I'm not fucking Mexican, Toby."

Toby's expression grew cold for a moment, and then he feigned a laugh and said, "Whatever, dude."

Then there was silence, a slow one that crept up on all of us, heavy and sinister.

Jess shivered. "I'm getting cold, are you, Liz?"

Lizzie, who'd been staring slack-jawed at this exchange, her cigarette ashy between her fingers, just nodded.

"Close your mouth," Jess hissed at Lizzie under her breath. Her eyes met mine in what felt like a moment of understanding, but then it was all over and the girls got up, brushed the grass off their candy-colored shorts and left.

"Jesus," Max mused, chuckling to himself. "That was intense, Connor."

"Shut up, Max," I said.

They all turned to stare at me. It felt like an eternity before I blinked and snapped back to life, playing it off like I was joking and slapped Max on the back. "Just kidding, man."

But I could feel Toby's cold gaze creeping onto me, a slow smirk forming at the corner of his lips. "Yeah, you were just kidding, Jack. Always just kidding. Such a fucking kidder, my man, Jack!"

"The fuck is wrong with you, Toby?" Max asked, laughing nervously.

Connor mumbled something under his breath.

"What'd you just say?" Toby snapped.

Connor slid his shades up his nose. "Nothing that concerns you," he said with a sarcastic grin, and then nodded at me. "You coming, Jack?"

I hesitated, looking between Max and Toby and Connor. Toby was staring straight at Connor now, getting that scary look again, and Max just looked confused.

"Yeah, I'm coming. See you guys later."

"Later, dude!" Max called.

As I was walking away I thought I could just faintly hear Toby murmur, "*Fucking faggot.*"

30

Dr. Phil was on, and Mom was watching intently. She had

her feet up on the coffee table, still wearing her ratty bathrobe even though it was nearly noon. But something was weird; I smelled the familiar scent of pot.

"Goddamn, where do they find these people?" she said. She flicked some ashes onto the rug. "Morons of the highest order, babe. Of course, this quack knows exactly what to say to them, anyone with half a brain could fix *their* issues." She took a long drag.

"Mom?" I asked cautiously, walking over to her. I put my hands on her shoulders and gave them a gentle squeeze. "Are you smoking weed, Mom?"

She took a long hit on what I could now see was a joint. "Hope you don't mind. Found it in your room while I was cleaning a bit. Don't tell your father." She winked and inhaled again, the thick smoke curling into the air.

I pulled my hands off her shoulders like they'd shocked me. "Mom. Please don't go through my stuff."

The circles under her eyes were deep and dark, as if she hadn't slept in weeks. "Now Jack, it's my duty as a mother to make sure you're not getting into any nasty business, like drugs or weapons or sex." She laughed dryly and then started to cough. "God forbid," she went on in between hacking chest coughs. "I don't want my beautiful son to end up anything but boring."

"Didn't you have a job interview this morning?" My eyes were fixated by the people on the screen with their sad, crumpled faces as a bald fat man drawled his pop psychology at them in his bumble-fuck accent.

"I needed a mental health day," she said, flicking the joint again. It irked me.

The audience of dumpy middle-aged people cooed and

cheered for their Texan messiah. I realized I was grinding my teeth.

I walked over and turned the TV off, grabbing the joint from her and putting it out in the clay shark ashtray I'd made for her. Gunther lifted his head up from his spot by the window, making an anxious groaning noise.

"Mom. It's almost afternoon and you're still sitting around in your robe watching trash TV and smoking *my* weed, for fuck's sake. The house is a mess, the dog needs a walk, the bills are still sitting on the fucking foyer, not getting paid. What the hell are you doing?"

Her smirk had twisted into a cold scowl. "Who do you think you are, your father?"

"Someone around here has to be an adult," I said. "Come on, Gunther."

But before I could reach my dog, she stood and blocked my path. She was so small, about a foot shorter than me, but she stared up at me and lowered her tone. "You don't get to talk to me like that, I'm your *mother*!" It was then I saw that her face was about to fall from the weight of her tears and pain, and in a second she had collapsed into my arms and was pulling me close, the smell of cheap weed and bad perfume overwhelming.

"Oh, Jack," she murmured. I let her hot tears soak my t-shirt as I lightly patted her back in an attempt at comfort, until I had to pull away. I stomped out of the house with Gunther in tow, clipping on his leash without giving her a second look while she sniffled and sobbed pathetically into her hands.

Walking outside into the fresh air, I took a deep breath. Old Gunther walked patiently by my side, tail wagging every now and then, never pulling ahead or dragging behind me even if he spotted a squirrel or another dog. Despite his arthritis, he kept up with me down the sidewalk of our bleak street, with its potholes and small, unkempt houses.

Me and Gunther, my guy, who I'd raised myself, the only reliable member of my family.

31

"Will it hurt?" I asked.

The burly man crouched down to my level and gently touched my bottom lip with his latex finger. "Only a pinch. Just take a deep breath and relax when I clamp you."

"It's gonna look sick," Connor whispered in my ear. He kissed my cheek. We stared at our reflection in the mirror of the piercing parlor, his head resting on my shoulder, eyes wide with excitement next to my uneasy stare.

"I'm such a pussy," I touched the spot on my lip about to be severed, as if wishing it luck in its final intact moments.

"Nah, you're just a little dramatic," Connor said. "Now this one, see?" He pushed aside a clump of hair to reveal a rook piercing in his ear. "This one hurt like a *bitch.* Got infected and everything."

"Oh thanks, that really makes me feel better."

"You sure you want to go through with this?" the piercing guy asked with mock melodrama, patting my shoulder.

"Yeah, just fucking do it."

"Alright, kid, open up."

He put the cold clamp down on my bottom lip and

took out the big needle. "Deep breaths, all the way in, all the way out." I squeezed my eyes shut. "*Just* relax." I felt the needle go through with a tight pinch and Connor started cheering like I'd scored a touchdown.

"Yes! You did it, Jack!"

"Ow," I said as the guy put in the ring.

"Just remember to use the cleaning stuff I gave you so it so it doesn't get infected," he said. After we paid him, he squinted hard at me and mumbled, "I'll be damned if you're a day over sixteen." He shook his head and walked into the backroom, thumbing his fat cash tip from Connor.

Connor took my hand, and we went outside into the bright sunlight, taking in the smell of greasy fast food cooking next door. "So, what are you gonna tell your Dad?"

"That a rattlesnake bit me and this was the only way to stop the bleeding."

"Nice. I just got a text from Jason Xiang—you know him, right?—about this party. His parents are out of town for the weekend. He lives on Cypress Road, across the street from the pawn shop. You want to head over there?"

Jason Xiang? Was he in our grade? How did Connor know all these people? "Nah, not really."

"He's got four ounces of weed," he said, reading his phone. "And an eight ball."

"Yeah, I guess we could stop by."

"It *would* be rude to refuse," Connor agreed, smiling at me. I kissed him with my swollen lip.

A car horn honked. I glanced up to see a beat-up Ford slowly driving past us, an old woman in the driver's seat shaking her head and scowling in our direction.

Connor flipped her off and he pulled my face close to

his, kissing me hard and heavy with tongue. She honked angrily, her shouts trailing behind her as her tires screeched against the concrete.

Connor just laughed with his head back. His arm had felt so good around my waist just moments earlier, and I'd felt so free, but now I pulled away. It was like that easy warmth between us had evaporated.

"Come on, Jack," he murmured, pulling me closer to him, but I shrugged him off.

"Not now."

"Jack," he said. "Are we gonna do this forever?"

"Please," I said. "Just not now."

We walked to the bus stop in silence.

It was always strange going out into public spaces, a sphere where we couldn't touch or smile at each other like we did when we were alone. Not without causing a nasty response. For a while it had been our unspoken agreement that everything between us only existed when we were back in the safety our bubble, away from anyone who might suspect us.

But lately he'd been getting increasingly annoyed with it. He'd been touching me out in public, acting bolder, more insistent that we just come out to everyone and let it be what it was.

"It's not a big deal, Jack," he'd said. "I know it's scary, but once you're honest with everyone and yourself, it's so freeing. We don't have to keep playing this game."

But I would picture Riley, left naked and bruised and alone in that hallway. I saw him behind my eyelids whenever I tuned out in class, when I turned a sharp corner in the hallway, when I dreamed at night. His long face and crooked smile would find their way into my brain even in my most peaceful moments alone with Connor, reminding me, warning me. It had only been a month since he'd been beaten up, but for some reason, it felt strange to talk about, even with Connor.

I felt it on the bus that day, in the way Connor stared out the window and barely spoke to me, that it was bugging him too. I wish I could tell him about the dreams I'd been having, the ones where a million hands were clutching my throat and choking me to death, or how the thought of someone seeing us together made my chest turn icy cold, like all the air had been sucked out of my lungs. But it felt like speaking about it would only make it more real.

When we arrived at Jason's, a red brick row house with a crumbling roof and creaky porch, a steady bass was pulsing through the walls. I rapped hard on the door and rang the bell three times, hearing yelling and excited screams inside.

The door opened and my mouth fell open.

"Jess?"

I barely recognized her. In the place of my best friend was a nineties grunge model. Her hair was messy and matted, pulled back into a bun on top of her head, dark roots bleeding through. Her lashes were thick with mascara, and her lips were painted bright red. She easily looked five years older, but tired under all the makeup. She stood there staring at me in mutual surprise, wearing ripped-up tights and a skintight black dress that hugged her thighs. Her automatic, friendly smile quickly fell into a grimace.

"Oh, hello, Jack," she said coolly, eyeing Connor and me warily. "Come in, I guess."

I stepped into a cloud of stale beer and cigarettes. "You know Jason?"

She just nodded and shrugged, sipping her drink. "Everyone knows Jason. He's running for SGA president."

"We have an SGA?" I was only half-kidding.

She tried to hide her smirk with her hand. "You want a beer? I'll get you one. Oh, and Toby asked if you were coming. He said he'd be upstairs in a minute." She walked off to the kitchen.

I was dumbfounded. I glanced over at Connor. "She's hanging out with *Toby*, now?"

"I guess they're friends now," Connor said. We watched a sketchy-looking couple dry hump in the stairway that led to the basement, where the party was raging down below.

I thought back to the last party, the way he'd been leering at her, and my stomach turned. "Do you think she's here for him? Like, they're on a *date* or something?"

"You know her better than I do. I'll meet you downstairs. Sounds like something's happening in the basement."

I headed into the kitchen where Jess was pouring beers. "You know I don't touch Natty Light."

Then her face broke out into a real smile, and she handed me my drink. "Cheers to that." She tapped her cup against mine. "That's why I poured you the good stuff." I smiled back. Her eyebrows shot up. "Did you get your lip pierced?"

"Oh, yeah, today, I was with Connor. I was…gonna send you a pic."

"Right," she said. We stood there awkwardly, sipping our beers, watching people come and go through the cramped room. "Well, see you later, I guess."

She pushed past me but I stepped in front of her, blocking her path. “Wait, Jess, we need to talk.”

“About what? There’s nothing more to talk about, Jack.”

“I miss you,” I blurted out. “Everything’s just been so weird lately, and I miss talking to you. I miss how we used to be.”

She lowered her gaze to the floor. “Me too.”

“I would do anything to take it back. I didn’t mean it.”

When she lifted her eyes, they were hard and cold. “You left me at that party alone, drunk, scared, *hurt*, remember? My girlfriends weren’t even there.”

“I know. I don’t know what else to do or say to make it better. How many more times do you want me to apologize before you’ll actually forgive me?”

She just stared at me and shook her head sadly. “Toby’s right, you *are* clueless about some things.”

“Oh, so you’re *friends* with Toby now? You guys *talk*?”

I regretted it the second it slipped out of my mouth.

“Don’t look at me like I’m some kind of loser because I’m hanging out with *your* friends, Jack!”

Some people were starting to watch us. I lowered my voice and leaned closer to her. “Jess, I didn’t mean it like that. Please.”

“I’m done here, Jack. Come talk to me when you’ve grown a pair.” She started to walk off, but then stopped, as if she’d forgotten something. “And by the way, your so-called ‘friends?’ Your ‘boys?’ They don’t even like you all that much.”

I chugged the rest of my beer after she stalked off, then wandered downstairs into the haze of the party. I had the urge to punch something, someone. Every single face I saw in the crowd made me angrier.

When I finally found Connor amid the chaos, he was doing lines of coke off a dusty coffee table covered in empty red solo cups, a strung-out girl sliding her hand up the back of his shirt. I stood there for a moment, and some asshole bumped into me and let out a rude, "Excuse you." Connor's head was tilted back, his eyes closed, mouth open like he was in a state of pure ecstasy.

I pushed past the girl and put a hand on his shoulder. I didn't care who was watching. "Hey, you okay?"

"Mmm," he said, wiping his nose in his sleeve and sniffing loudly. "Everything's good, man." He started giggling, leaning down to do another line. I pushed his head away.

"Hey," I said, trying to laugh with him. "I think that's enough."

But he resisted, shoving me back. "No, I'm good. I'm good," he said, and snorted another line, starting to make a third one with someone's credit card. A few more girls were coming over now, all of them completely coked out. They were community college girls, way too old to be putting their hands all over Connor.

"That looks like good shit," one said.

"Can we get some?" asked another, leaning her head against Connor's shoulder and stroking his bicep. "You have nice arms."

"Hey Connor, come upstairs. I've got something better," I said. I gently tugged at his sleeve.

"Even better than this?" he asked. He sniffled loudly and wiped his nose. One of the girls nipped at his ear. "Excuse me ladies, I'll be right back."

I managed to get him upstairs, though he was shaking and kept looking around the room and biting at his lip.

"Come on, man," I said. "Let's go back to your place. I think you're good for tonight."

"Oh hey, Jack, Connor, nice of you to join us."

I froze. Toby. And next to him, this kid I kind of recognized, who must've been Jason Xiang. He was wearing a tank top that read: *Sometimes I drink water to surprise my liver,* and someone's lipstick kiss mark was on his cheek. My arm was linked through Connor's. I slowly disentangled myself, but Connor just moved in to give Toby a hug.

"Hey Jason," Connor said. "Toby! Good shit downstairs. Really good."

"Yeah?" said Toby. "I can tell you like it. We saw you doing some. You do know you owe me and Jason $50 for those lines you just did, right?"

There was an awkward pause, and then Toby started laughing and slapped him on the back. "I'm just playing, man! Good to see you. You and Jack have been pretty elusive these days."

I tried to read Toby's expression, but he was wearing a pair of dark sunglasses, the kind he loved to wear even indoors.

"Been keeping busy," said Connor. He sniffled joyously, high as a kite, before turning to Max. "Your air-conditioning is on point, man. Really top-notch electrical work in here."

"Thanks," Jason said with a chuckle. "We need it, with the smoke-shows we got downstairs. Did you see those girls, Connor? Anything that interested you in particular?"

"I'm gonna take him home now," I said.

Toby lifted his glasses just enough so I could see the bottom of his eyes. "You do that, Jack. You do that." Then he smirked, and it made my skin crawl.

Just as I started leading Connor out the door, I heard Toby say my name once more and turned to look at him. He gave me a sarcastic thumbs-up.

"Nice piercing, brah!"

32

That next morning was Dad's fortieth birthday. I got up early to go the Mini Mart with Mom to buy streamers, paper plates, balloons, and an ice cream cake—all red, white and star-spangled banner blue. We made scrambled eggs and bacon while Dad snored away upstairs, recovering from what I assumed to be a hangover. But when he finally stumbled downstairs in his ripped-up blue t-shirt and boxers, he wasn't the least bit bleary-eyed. He was whistling, fucking *whistling* at ten a.m., stirring sugar into his coffee as if this were any other weekend, clean-shaven and alert.

"Hey Dad," I said cautiously, pouring myself a cup. "You feeling alright?"

He nodded to some beat inside his head. Then he patted my arm and smiled at me. "Never been better, Jack. Never been better."

"Happy Birthday, Jim!"

Mom ran up and squeezed him tight, causing him to spill some coffee down his shirt. To my surprise he didn't snap something nasty at her. He only said, "Whoa there!" with a hearty chuckle.

"Good morning to you too, beautiful!" He kissed her cheek and they both smiled at me. There they were, arm in arm, a portrait of marital, suburban bliss.

Was I still high from last night?

"What's wrong, Jack?" Dad asked, murmuring his approval of the brew to Mom in between coffee sips. He walked over and thumped me on the back, gently. "Cheer up, kid. Your old man's forty today."

"Every day is a good day," Mom chanted blissfully.

Resolved that I was either still dreaming, tripping, or had awakened in some alternate universe, I spent the rest of the morning helping Mom decorate the backyard while Dad grilled hot dogs and burgers, sizzling smoke that smelled like summer barbecues and reminded me of childhood.

As we sat at the picnic table to eat, Dad announced he had big news for us. Mom clapped her hands with excitement.

"As of today," he said, looking us straight in the eye. "I have quit drinking."

I glanced at Mom, waiting for her to roll her eyes and scoff, and then back at Dad. But his expression was serious.

"Well, I'm proud," Mom said. She raised her plastic cup in a toast.

They looked at me expectantly.

"That's...that's great, Dad."

"I mean it this time," he said. "I know I've made a lot of promises to you both, I know I've messed up and let you both down—"

"Let's not dwell on the past, love," Mom said briskly.

In the middle of the meal, which I'd barely touched, I excused myself and went upstairs to my room and lit a cigarette.

I knew I should quit. I knew they could kill me, after first making my voice raspy and hard like Mom's, and I knew I smelled like an ashtray half of the time. I should probably switch to electronic cigarettes, try to wean myself off. But then I'd get restless again, and angry, and I'd reach for a cigarette. It didn't help that my house smelled like them.

I watched the sun fall against the leaves of the palm trees in our backyard, their trunks drooping and crooked. It was cooler than usual, and my skin relished the sun that wasn't beating down on me for a change. I lit my bong.

The door opened and Mom stood there, arms crossed, a huge frown on her face.

"You might want to stop being rude and come downstairs to celebrate your father's birthday," she said in that sickly-sweet voice she used when she was pissed.

I took a hit off my bong and she scoffed.

"Jack, really? Do you really have to do that in here? You're stinking up the whole house." She walked over to my window and opened it, letting in the hot air.

"I'm taking lessons from you."

"Excuse me?"

"Look, I'm not going back downstairs."

"And why not?"

I took another long hit. There she was in her clean blouse and jean shorts, trying so hard to be the picture of normality.

"Because I think you and Dad are completely full of shit."

She was silent for a moment. Her face contorted into a grimace and for a second I thought she might reach over and hit me. But then she stormed out of the room and slammed the door, leaving me alone with my bong and a mixture of anger and guilt in the pit of my stomach.

I tried calling Jess. No answer. She'd posted new pictures online of her with Skye and her friends, dolled-up, drunk, dancing, and looking happier than I'd seen her in forever. Before all of this, she would have come over, played video games and eaten popsicles on my lawn and laughed it off, my weirdo parents. We would have walked for miles around this town of broken dreams, past sidewalks full of holes and bumps, strip malls coated in garish colors, minivans and SUVs roasting in their gummy lots. We would have talked for hours or spent hours saying nothing at all.

Something pinched at my nose. *Damn.* I was going to cry. I let a few tears trickle out, wetting my cheeks, then brushed them aside and took a deep breath. I would call Connor. I'd go over there, and he'd fuck me and make me forget everything except for the smell of his warm skin and the feel of his body.

Maybe Jess had finally found her place after all, a place that didn't need or involve me. Maybe I should just take the hint already and leave her alone for good.

I went over to Connor's on Sunday morning. We watched our favorite movies back to back, huddled on the couch with my head on his chest. Marlon Brando and Al Pacino. He understood my love of these men, their rugged handsomeness and their sharp wits. He ran his fingers through my hair, my scalp tingling and my body filled up to the brim with warmth.

We sat on the patio smoking fresh weed, making out to a little rock, a little trap music.

"Where have you been?" Mom asked me that evening, grinning as I came downstairs after a day filled with everything Connor, the kind of day that left me feeling recharged and peaceful. She was in the kitchen wiping down wet dishes. My mother, cleaning, of all things. Dad's mess of a birthday party seemed to have been forgotten, or at least forgiven. I reached around her to grab a soda. "You look happy," she said. I shrugged.

She started adjusting the collar of my shirt. "You know why I named you Jack?"

I rolled my eyes. "After Grandpa Jack. And the old Hollywood guy. I know, Mom."

She sighed. "Yes, Jack Burns, the comedian and actor. Funny, handsome, so Hollywood glamour. Not unlike you." She kissed my cheek.

"Okay, Mom, thanks."

I checked my reflection in the hallway mirror. I'd left my hair un-gelled in the front, but I looked good. I felt good.

"You been hanging out with that cutie you brought home?"

I flinched. "Huh?"

"Oh, *you* know," she said, wagging her eyebrows at me. "That nice boy you brought here recently, Connor, I think it was? He was definitely a dish."

"*Mom*," I said. "Stop it."

"Stop what?"

"Stop being…creepy. He's way too young for you, anyway."

She smiled this slow, knowing smile. "But not too young for *you*."

"What?" I turned away so she couldn't see the look on my face. "What are you talking about?

"Stop pretending like I'm an idiot, Jack," she said more seriously. She moved over to me me and put an arm on my shoulder, which I shrugged off. "You're my son. I know you better than you think."

Something caught in the back of my throat, a tangle of words I wanted to say. I said nothing as she wrapped her arms around me and pulled me into a hug. Nothing when she kissed my forehead and gave me that look, that look that said she *knew*, and all I could do was nod and pull away from her and leave the room before I started crying.

She *knew*.

33

I sat on the kitchen counter, drinking down one of Connor's protein shakes. It tasted gritty and sweet, like sandpaper in a smoothie.

"How do you drink this shit every day?"

He shrugged and continued rummaging through the cabinets, organizing things, putting food away. "Hand me that bag, would you?"

For the next few minutes I helped him unload five heavy bags of groceries into the lavish designer kitchen. I loved being in there, with its chrome fixtures and all those top-of-the-line appliances. It was such a nice change from my house—so immaculate, so clean, so nice for the sake of being nice.

"I guess your uncle doesn't need to hire a housekeeper with you around."

He didn't smile. "He's a good guy."

"Hey, I didn't mean it like that."

He chewed his fingernail and pulled a pack of cigarettes from his bag. "I know you didn't." But he didn't look at me.

Feeling uncomfortable, I wandered over to the living room to check out the home entertainment system and the giant aquarium full of tropical fish. I loved the way the wood floors felt against my bare feet. Connor's house was huge and beautiful, full of cool little things like heated floorboards in the master bathroom and a popcorn machine next to the flat-screen TV. There were tons of pictures everywhere of friends and family with Connor's uncle, a friendly-looking guy with roughish features and the same grin as his nephew. Alvaro. I'd met him before. As far as I understood it, he was this big deal tech guy who'd worked for several of the biggest start-ups out west. Why he'd moved out here, to this shithole of a town, I still didn't quite get.

But when he came home and I was there, he'd always say "hello" to me politely and ask me about my day. And it was nice, having that kind of normalcy, even if I was never sure how to act around Connor with him there, if he ever suspected anything. But he was "married to his job," as Connor liked to say, so we mostly had the house to ourselves.

Connor wasn't in any of the photos that I could see, but I didn't want to ask about it. And then it caught my eye: an elegantly gold-framed picture on the mantle of the fireplace of a pretty young couple and a little boy with shaggy black hair and bright green eyes.

I picked up the picture carefully, as if it were fragile and might easily break. I held it up a little and called out to him, "Hey, is this you?"

He squinted, then went back to looking through his bag. "Yeah."

"Are these your parents?"

"Yup."

I put the picture back in its place and studied it. The woman had flowing hair like a black waterfall and a dreamy smile. The man was much darker than her in complexion, broad-shouldered and handsome like his son.

"Do you…ever talk to them?"

"Nope."

And then he added, "Never will."

"Why?"

He snorted. "They don't give a shit about me, whether I live or die. They made that pretty clear. Why should I give a shit about them and their bullshit lives?" He was rinsing the glass I'd been drinking out of, fiercely scrubbing out the protein gunk.

I walked over to him and put my hands on his shoulders, but he kept at it, then filed it away in the dishwasher with a loud clang and began washing his hands with the same ferocity. Steam was rising from the tap.

I reached over and turned it off. His hands were bright red.

"Don't do that," I said gently.

"Don't ask me about them."

"Sorry."

He shook his head and his shoulders relaxed. "No, it's okay," he said, his tone gentler. "You knew they were in prison, but you didn't know that."

"Can I ask…where were you before? Before you lived with your uncle? I know you said you were in the foster system, but where exactly?"

He laughed shortly. "What are you, a fucking journalist?"

"I'm sorry. I'm just curious. I mean, I tell you everything about me, about my family. I barely know anything about you. And you just—you just always seem so together. So impossibly…perfect. I know, that sounds dumb. If you want me to stop, just say it."

He finally turned around to face me. I expected some anger, some agitation, but he looked like he'd been trying not to cry. Then he flinched and straightened out his expression, looking away again like eye contact was physically painful.

"It's okay, man. I get it. I'll leave now if you want," I told him.

He took a deep breath and cleared his throat. "No. I know you've heard rumors. How I punched a principal at St. Francis, how I started riots, sold drugs, slept with every girl under the sun. But all of them are a crock of shit. They don't even come close."

He opened his pack of cigarettes and stuck one in his mouth, then opened the sliding door to the backyard. "You coming or what?"

I followed him outside into the cool haze of dusk, a dull lullaby of crickets like surround sound, the sky a milky blue. We sat in the grass and stared at the lush expanse of lawn before us, at the looming pine trees with their scarred trunks.

He lit his cigarette, not offering me one like he usually did. "Okay, fire away. Ask me anything you want."

It had been so different when he'd said that to me up in his bedroom. Now he wasn't even looking at me. I kept my gaze on the trees, feeling hesitant about prying. I'd never seen him like this before, and it scared me.

"I did get kicked out of St. Francis," he said. "Then I transferred here, and it was all because of my uncle. He helped me when no one else would. He moved here for me. He can do that with his job. He can work anywhere."

"Why did you get kicked out?"

He took a long drag off his cigarette before answering. "I beat the shit out of this guy. He wouldn't leave this kid alone."

"What kid?"

"Just this kid at school. This kid who wouldn't stand up for himself. Who couldn't stand up for himself. And seeing that happen, day after day, eventually I just snapped. I punched that asshole dead in the mouth, and I just kept going. I couldn't stop. It was like this wild rush, and I blacked out or something. All I remember is feeling my fist connect with his face, how good that felt. I fucking *liked* it. Can you believe that? But then some teachers got involved, tried to break us up, and apparently, I elbowed one of them in the face. I didn't mean to. I really didn't. But those fucking teachers, man. They'd seen it. They'd seen what he did to that kid, every single day, and they never did or said anything."

"So…you transferred here. Why here?"

"It was the only school in the area that would take me. My uncle just wants me to finish high school, you know? This is like, my last shot, short of getting a GED." He laughed even though it wasn't funny. "He and my dad, they came to America when they were little kids. But my grandparents moved back to Santiago, to be with family before they…before they died. And my parents got caught up in some shit, meanwhile. And then they went to prison. And by that time my uncle was back in Santiago, organizing the funeral for my grandparents, doing everything, while my fucking parents were at the federal courthouse for months, begging to be let off easy. And I was in the system. With no one. I eventually contacted him, my uncle. I tracked him down online, found his LinkedIn, sent him a bunch of emails. I was so desperate. And I asked him to get me out. And he did. He came back for me. So, I kind of owe him my life."

I tried to choose my words with care. "Where exactly did you live before you lived with your uncle?"

"A group home."

"What was that like?"

He scoffed. "Fucking pizza party every day, man. Up to my ass in pretty girls. Heaven on Earth."

I couldn't think of something else to ask, so I just sat in silence as we listened to the crickets for a while before he spoke.

"I've been in and out of a bunch of different group and foster homes pretty much my whole life. My parents got arrested pretty early on. But there's stuff I haven't told you. Like, in one of the foster homes, it was five of us kids. The woman in charge had this boyfriend, this older guy, this fucking asshole who lived there and acted like he owned the place. He liked to slap us and her around for like, everything. He pushed one of the kids down the stairs once and broke her leg. For some asinine reason, I'm sure. I lived there for three years."

He took a hard drag on his cigarette. The tip glowed like a firefly.

"He tried some shit with me, some of it I don't care to remember. He liked to touch me at weird times, in strange places. He also liked to beat me with a belt. I knew he liked it, fucking *loved* it, that sicko. And he liked hitting me in particular. I would try to avoid him, but he always found some way to get at me when I was alone and defenseless. So at school I'd go to the weight room and pump iron every day, until everything burned. I never got that big, but I got stronger. One day I came home and he was shoving one of the kids around, and screaming at them. I yelled at him to stop and he went over to hit me. So, I grabbed him by the throat and shoved him against the wall. Told him if he ever put his hands on me or one of the other kids again I would fucking murder him. I would tear his throat out. It was like I had this superhuman strength inside me all of a sudden. I'll never forget that look on his face. Pure terror. They had me placed in another group home, but for the last few days I was there he didn't go near me, wouldn't even look at me. I was fourteen."

He flicked the butt on the ground and stomped on it, then turned to look at me. "So, what else you want to know, Jack?" Then his voice softened. "I'm not perfect, okay? I'm not even close."

"I can tell you my earliest memory," I said suddenly. The words just spilled out of me. I wanted him to keep going, to tell me everything, but I wanted to share something too. I hugged my knees to my chest, suddenly feeling lonely, even sitting here with Connor. "I was probably like, three or four? Three, I think. My dad was really drunk, really angry. He was going to get fired. I remember that. My mom was mad too. They were throwing shit. There was broken glass. And screaming. So much screaming. And my mom, she must've been so scared. She just grabbed me and threw me in the car, and she drove away. We went to this motel, this place that looked like a palace. I thought it was a castle. Like she'd saved me from him and taken me somewhere far away. Eventually he came to get us and I was screaming and begging not to leave that shitty motel. I wanted to live there forever. Part of me wishes we did."

Then I felt Connor's hand on top of mine, our fingers interweaving. And we just sat like that for a while, him smoking another cigarette, me staring out into the endless twilight.

34

Toby wouldn't stop kicking my chair.

It was nine a.m. on a Monday and I was bleary from lack of sleep. Kick, kick, kick. I turned around and frowned at him, mouthing, *Knock it off.* He just grinned. I gave him the finger before turning back around.

I was trying to concentrate, I really was. I liked English, especially Mrs. Flores. She was young but really knew her stuff. She'd go on tangents about Gothic literature or some other cool thing, and while most of the class threw things at each other I'd sit there entranced, amazed at the scope and history of it all, wondering if I was the only one in this class who appreciated that she was too good for this shitty school. Today she was talking about the Harlem Renaissance.

Kick, kick, kick. I tried to focus, tried to ignore it and take notes. Finals were coming up and I didn't want to fuck up again and end up back in this section with all the morons.

Mrs. Flores turned off the lights and flipped on the projector, showing us slides of Harlem in the 1930s, explaining how black people used art and music and literature to challenge racist stereotypes. It was so cool. It had absolutely nothing to do with our curriculum-mandated reading, but she never seemed to care and no one ever noticed. Every now and then her eyes would pass over me diligently writing things down. She'd smile at me, and I'd smile back. It was like our little secret, my own private lesson while she spoke to a bored audience and pretended she was lecturing at a private university. I wondered how she'd ended up in this shithole.

Kick, kick, kick, *kick*. The kicks got harder, more intense. I turned around and punched Toby's desk. He just laughed, loudly, enjoying himself. "Stop it," I said.

He smirked and turned to Jerry Rudoy. They exchanged an eye-roll and chuckled at my expense. Toby continued kicking, steadily and gently. "That a better rhythm for you? That how you like it?" he asked, moaning softly. Jerry cackled.

Mrs. Flores cleared her throat loudly. "Can I help you, boys?"

"No," Toby said, still looking at me. "You're good."

"Toby won't stop kicking my chair," I said, then realized how whiny I sounded. Someone laughed.

Mrs. Flores sighed deeply. "And why are we having trouble keeping our bodies to ourselves, Toby?"

Toby shrugged. "I think you should ask Jack that." Jerry and a couple of his new buddies burst out laughing.

"Well, if you don't quit being a smartass, I'm gonna have to ask you to leave my classroom and spend the rest of the period sitting outside Principal Oliver's office. Would you like that, Toby?"

Toby slid his foot out from under my chair and put his hands up. "Continue, please. I'm sorry to have interrupted your stimulating lecture." More laughter rippled through the room.

"There's no need to be rude, Toby," Mrs. Flores said. She glanced at the clock on the wall wistfully, as if reluctantly accepting the inevitable bullshit that came with teaching this class.

"What the fuck was that?" I snapped at Toby the moment the bell rang and everyone was pushing to get out.

Toby just laughed and waved at Jerry and company. "Don't worry about it. We were just fucking around."

"Bullshit, Toby."

He put his arm around my shoulder and shook me. "God, you're so sensitive! Chill out, man. I'm just messing with you. That class is boring. Anyway, you want to come smoke with me and Max?"

He kept walking, but I stopped in the hallway, ignoring the asshole Brett that bumped into me on purpose.

"Faggot!" Brett sang, his deep voice resonating down the hall.

That stopped me cold.

"Toby," I said. "What the hell?"

He looked at me and shrugged. We stood there like that for a moment, silence filling the emptying halls.

I walked numbly to my next class, the weight of my backpack feeling heavier than ever, like I was treading through deep mud. But I had to focus. I had to pay attention. I couldn't let them get to me.

I had to finish junior year.

35

"Wakey, wakey." I woke to Connor leaning over me, his hoodie pulled up over his head, bright green eyes staring into mine.

"Hey," I said, pulling on one of the strings hanging down. I had never been so happy to wake up.

"Hey." He leaned in and kissed me.

"What time is it?" The clock read noon. It felt so good to sleep in on Saturday, and at his house no less.

He grinned. "I got you something."

I started to sit up as he tossed something into my lap. A bagel with egg and bacon wrapped in paper.

"Damn, thanks," I said. "You are by far the world's best alarm clock."

He laid down next to me and pulled a fucking protein shake out of his bag.

"Is that all you're gonna eat?" I asked, tearing into my sandwich.

"Hey, hey, crumbs," he said, handing me a napkin.

"Seriously, do you ever try *real* protein?"

He shrugged and took a sip. "I don't eat that shit until afternoon, man."

"You are so weird."

"I can get weirder."

"Oh yeah?"

"Yeah."

"Then let's get out of here."

So we did. Connor had the keys to his uncle's souped-up Jeep for the week, a prospect that absolutely amazed me. I'd learned to drive on Dad's clunky old Kia, and not very well. We could go anywhere, do anything.

Connor looked good behind the wheel, looked so right wearing his designer black sunglasses, a black tank top, and a pair of board shorts. He steered with one hand, and I sat back and let the sunlight hit my face as we sped down the highway, Yeezy's latest tracks blasting through the speakers. And man, they were sick speakers.

"One day I'm gonna have a car like this," I said, watching Burro Hills fade away in the rearview mirror.

"You and me both."

"As long as I don't end up a total drunk deadbeat like my dad. Or fail out of school." I laughed, but he didn't say anything. It was hard to gauge his expression from behind those shades.

We were getting closer to the ocean, the air balmier and the breeze stronger.

"I know this place," Connor said. "It's a little cove. No one goes there."

Hours later, we sat in the warm sand, reveling in the hot and salty breeze of the beach.

"You wanna go in?" Connor asked, smiling at me from behind his Ray Bans.

I said sure. I'd do anything he wanted to do.

The water was cold at first and jolted my nerves awake. We waded in deeper, past the breakers that pounded against our bodies as they smacked the shoreline. The ocean was navy blue against thin clouds suspended in the bright sky. I went under, letting the water fill my ears and drown my thoughts and senses, then surfaced and swallowed the fresh air, so much cleaner and easier to breathe than the dead, dull air of Burro Hills.

"Let's never go back," I said.

Connor laughed and splashed me. "What would we do?"

"Sleep under the stars, learn to eat sea grass." I splashed him back, harder.

He pulled me in close and kissed me.

I leaned my head back and let the sun hit me full on, heat sliding across my face. "You know," I said. "I always hated vacations."

"Why?"

"Well, not the vacation itself. More the time in between that you spend thinking about going home, back to bland, dull real life."

"Back to the grind," Connor echoed. "Back to nothing."

"Yup."

We swam around for a while in silence, letting the cold water engulf us with each rolling wave until it felt as warm as the air to our skin.

Afterwards we dried off and spread out on one big towel, watching the sun begin its descent to the fringes of the sea. Connor sighed and laid his head on his hands, his face towards me. Even in the fading light, he was so beautiful, innocent even. I couldn't take it anymore.

"Connor, why do you like me?" I asked. I'd been holding the question inside for so long the words nearly burst out.

He frowned. "What do you mean?"

"I mean, why me? Of all the…people at school."

I sat up and played with the sand, letting it fall through my fingers and breaking apart the little rocks of them that stuck together.

He was thoughtful for a moment and then said, "Because you're beautiful."

I felt my face get warm. "I'm not a model or anything."

"No, no. That's not what I meant." He looked me in the eye. "I mean don't get me wrong, you're definitely easy on the eyes, cute, handsome…" I laughed bashfully and he laughed too, reaching his hand over to stroke mine. "But I mean you're…I don't know…you just *get* things. You have this energy; fuck, I can't explain this very well. You see the world as it truly is and understand the pain of it, past the bullshit and the hype, behind the lies and forced smiles and fake laughs. You're a real person Jack. You're beautiful."

The emotions I experienced then and there, on that

beach, were so intense, so indescribably exciting and strange and blissful and scary as all hell that I kissed him. I wrapped my hands around his neck and pulled his hair, moving on top of him, our naked stomachs pressed together, his breathing growing hard and fast. I kissed his hot, wet skin tenderly, noting his surprise at my sudden aggressive maneuver, and we shed what remained of our clothes and made love right there on that empty beach, under a fiery setting sun.

36

Mom was more restless than I'd ever seen her. That glazed look in her eyes had been replaced by a permanent scowl, her lips smashed together. She no longer wore any makeup, just sat at the kitchen table or in front of the TV in her bathrobe, chain-smoking, biting her nails. Pacing from room to room.

Dad was going out more and more and coming home less and less.

I tried to do little things for her. I brought her flowers, a bouquet of white lilies, and she lit up for a moment and touched my cheek. But just like that she was back to watching re-runs of *Wheel of Fortune* and *Judge Judy* from morning to night. She didn't laugh like she used to or make comments about all the people on-screen. She barely spoke.

Gunther seemed to sense the change. When I got home he looked up at me expectantly, hungrily. Mom wasn't feeding him anymore or buying him food. I started leaving him in the yard while I was out so he could relieve himself, even though I was worried about the coyotes. I could hear them screaming and moaning at night, mimicking the cries of babies.

Then one Sunday morning I woke to the smell of blueberry muffins, classic rock reverberating through the house. I rolled over and pulled the covers over my head, trying to go back to sleep. No such luck. Whatever Billy Joel concert or bed and breakfast had infiltrated my home was clearly not going away anytime soon.

I pulled on a t-shirt and sweats and hobbled sleepily downstairs. What I saw made me question whether or not I was still dreaming.

There was Mom, dressed in a plum-colored pantsuit and a crisp white blouse, pearls laced around her neck. *Baking.* A tray of fresh-baked muffins sat cooling on the counter, and she was now using some fancy device to make tea. Worst of all, she was humming along to the music. Mom rarely listened to music that wasn't coming from a TV commercial.

"Mom?" I asked, cautiously making my way downstairs.

She turned and smiled at me. Her face was all dolled up, hair tumbling down her shoulders in flowing waves. Holy shit, my mother was beautiful. When was the last time I'd seen her looking like this?

"Oh, hi sweetie, I'm making ginger tea," she said. "There's fresh muffins, and I can whip up some eggs if you'd like."

We had eggs? I'd been surviving on fast food and whatever I could eat at school or Connor's house.

"Uh, okay," I said. "Mom…are you…alright?"

She blew tenderly on the muffins and plucked one out of the tray, holding it out to me like this was normal, like she did things like make her son muffins and fucking ginger tea in the morning. "Just in a good mood," she said. "I have an interview in a few hours, and oh, Daddy said he was bringing me a surprise tonight." She lit up at that, like some love-struck schoolgirl. "Eat something, honey, you look like you haven't in days."

Mom had been somewhat like this before. When I was little, she was always baking, the radio playing soft rock, the window open, the smells of eucalyptus and sweetgum filling the kitchen. Those were the good days, the days when Dad didn't get home until after midnight, and I was usually asleep by the time they were fighting and screaming and things were breaking. Mom's wails were muffled by the walls and ceiling.

I sat at the table and picked at a blueberry muffin. Gunther was laying under my feet, tail wagging happily. Maybe I'd done too much acid and ended up in an alternate reality.

Mom kept humming, running her fingers along her pearls. I didn't even know she owned them.

I finally swallowed hard and made myself speak. "Mom," I said. "We need to talk."

"About what?"

"Can you please sit down?"

That's when I noticed that she wouldn't stop moving. She was scrubbing the counter, blowing on the muffins, checking the fridge, opening and closing cabinets. It was like someone had disabled her "off" switch. Even in her pretty pantsuit and pearls, she was scaring me.

"Mom, listen. I know you've been bummed out lately, but there's some things you really need to do. I'm happy about your interview, but you need to remember to show up on time. And make sure to walk Gunther while I'm at school, and buy groceries and dog food regularly, and lay off the cigarettes, okay? I've been really worried about you."

She wasn't listening. She was still buzzing about, humming like she couldn't hear me, munching her muffin, crumbs all over her blouse.

The kettle whistled. She clapped her hands like it was the most delightful sound she'd ever heard.

"Mom!" I shouted.

"Yes, my love?" she said.

"Can you please listen to me? For one second? You're seriously creeping me out right now!"

For a moment the kitchen was quiet, save for the rock music and the sound of Gunther sighing. Then she glared at me, dusting the crumbs from her blouse. "You know, I haven't seen your friend Jess around here lately. You two get in a fight or something?"

I threw my hands up. "What the hell does that have to do with anything I just said?"

"Watch your language, please," she snapped. And then her voice went dark. "I miss having her around. She was so sweet, such a nice girl. You know, your dad thought that about me when we met. He thought I was such a nice girl, but now…" She fumbled in her pocket and pulled out her trusty cigarettes, lighting one with shaky hands. "Now it's like I don't even exist. Like nothing I do matters. Well, how can I make it matter, Jack? How?"

Before I could even fathom how to answer that, Dad

powered in. His keys went clank, his boots went bang against the wall as he kicked them off, and his voice went boom. Gunther let out a pitiful whine.

Perfect.

"How's my beautiful family this morning?" he called out to us. He slapped his bloated belly and laughed and hiccupped. I could barely look at him. He'd been drinking hard. That was obvious. His face was bright red, and he was smacking his lips together like he'd just eaten something delicious. It was nauseating beyond belief. "Oh." He stopped, as if he just noticed me and mom sitting there, and the blueberry muffins, and the kitchen full of groceries. "Well shit, Ellie. I haven't seen this in a while."

She smiled thinly. "Me baking? Would you like one, Jim? They're fresh from the oven."

He laughed. "Well, I haven't seen you doing much of anything other than watching *Maury* re-runs in your bathrobe all day. And I'd *love* one, thanks baby." He plucked one off the table and took a huge bite.

Mom wasn't smiling anymore. She put out her cigarette in her mug of tea with a *hiss*.

"Things going well at the bar, Jim? You bring home enough tip money that'll possibly help cover this month's electricity bill?"

Gunther whined from under the table. I reached down to scratch him behind the ear.

"Well, you know, Ellie, at least I *have* a job. And at least I'm making more than minimum wage. If you're so worried about the lights getting cut off, why don't you go back down to the grocery store and beg for your cashier gig back, huh? Maybe the movie theater will let you sell tickets again. Maybe Jack can get another job after school, pitch in around here for once instead of running around all day with his friends. What do you say, Jack?"

There was so much of this I could take. "I'm going out."

I started to stand, but Dad moved to block my way. "YOU SIT DOWN!"

"Jim!" Mom shrieked. "Don't scream in his ear!"

"We are having a family financial discussion!" Dad yelled. Gunther shoved his nose against my knee and groaned, tail wagging nervously.

"This is not a discussion, and this is not a family!" Mom screamed back. "This is not a home! Look at this shit! Look at this cheap, shitty floor you can't even be bothered to replace!" She fell to her knees and started tearing up the linoleum, a wild look in her eyes.

"Don't, Ellie!" Dad dashed over and grabbed her roughly by the arm, and she elbowed him hard in the gut.

"Both of you just stop it!" I shouted. I tried to push him off her, and he lost his balance and tumbled to the torn linoleum, knocking over a chair and the plate with the muffins. It shattered instantly, and he cursed loudly as Mom screeched as loudly as the kettle. Gunther yelped and darted across the room.

"Oh!" Mom's hands flew to her mouth. She looked around, eyes wide, tears streaming down her face, as if she'd suddenly realized where she was. "It was perfect! Everything was so perfect!" she cried. She hurried to clean up the broken plate. I tried to help her, but she snatched the pieces away from my hands, nearly cutting them in the process.

"Jesus, Mom! Let me help you!"

Dad was panting as he struggled to get up. I could tell by his face that the room was spinning, and that he might puke soon. It was nothing I wanted to deal with. So I turned to the door.

"Just where the hell do you think you're going, Jack?" he bellowed, pointing at me. Mom was still crying about the stupid cheap plate from the Dollar Store, moaning about the surprise she wouldn't get now. I couldn't take it anymore.

"Out," I said. "I'm going out, and you both can sort your shit out while I'm gone."

"Jack!" Mom gasped.

"You do not speak to us like that!" Dad growled. He was getting to his feet now, but stumbling, sliding on the floor that Mom had just mopped.

I pushed past Gunther, who was now whining and panting wildly in front of me, and grabbed my keys and wallet. Right as I was about to open the door, Dad shouted at me: "Where are you going? Hang out with that loser buddy of yours?"

The words just tumbled out before I could stop them. "No, Dad, I need to go *fuck* that loser buddy of mine."

They both stared at me, frozen in time for a moment, and I hurried out of there before I could hear any more from them.

37

We laid on his bed, watching the ceiling fan make its slow, deliberate spins as it rained down cool air on our faces.

"One day we'll go to Bermuda," he said, his hand resting on my chest. "We'll get on a jet and fly so far away from here."

"We'll drink piña coladas in the water," I added, smiling at the idea.

"We'll get so drunk the waves will probably wash us away," he said.

I sighed. "I hope they do."

He turned to look at me, searching my face for an explanation.

"No, I didn't mean it…it's just," I said. "Nevermind."

We lay there in the cool stillness for a while longer, the blades of the fan making a low whooshing sound against the static air.

"How's your dad doing?" he asked, breaking the silence.

I shrugged. "My father is an alcoholic bartender."

"My father's in maximum-security prison."

"Two fucked-up fathers. No wonder we're complete degenerates. We never had a chance." I laughed, but Connor didn't.

Instead he sat up on his elbows and leaned over me, his eyes meeting mine with a ferocity I'd never seen before. "Don't say that. Not even if you're joking. Don't ever say that."

I must have looked shocked because he reached over and lightly stroked my face, massaging his nails through my scalp. "You know it isn't true," he said. "That's what they want you to think, what they want you to believe. And the second you start believing it, you're fucked."

I reached over to hold his hand, pulling his body

towards me. He draped over me like a warm blanket, his stomach pressing into mine as he exhaled.

"I believed it once," he said into my ear. I could feel the vibrations in his voice all the way at the bottom of my spine. "I almost gave up completely, lost interest in living. I felt so disconnected from my body, like I was just this entity floating inside it, and it was a shell that needed to be taken off. Do you know what it's like, to have someone overpowering you, hurting you, beating you, and there's nothing you can do about it?" Something was cracking through that normally tough exterior.

I pulled his warm skin closer to me, pressing my lips to his ear. "I'll never let anyone hurt you like that ever again. I promise."

I felt his hot tears on my skin. It shook me to my core, feeling his brokenness. I repeated the vow I'd just made in my head, over and over like a prayer, rubbing his back like my mom did to me when I was little. How did he even survive as kid without someone there to love him, to protect him?

How could anyone?

38

His sleeping face was buried in my navy blue pillow. Sunlight poured in through my window, shattering across his bare skin like broken snowflakes. I lay frozen, head groggy with sleep, my heart starting a steady drum line as I realized where we were.

We'd ended up at my house last night after spending the day at his. We'd been high, completely zonked out on weed, smoking and taking shots of whiskey until we ending up passing out in my bed.

My house.

Fuck.

I tried to attune my ears to the noises of the house, praying no one else was home. Connor's soft breathing was like a lullaby tempting me back to sleep, but I was too wired now, too amped. I covered him with my sheet and walked softly to the door. Someone banged into it loudly, and I jumped. "Who is it?" I called. No one answered. I opened it slowly, relieved to find a fuzzy face staring up at me expectantly.

"Oh hey buddy, it's just you." I crouched down and gave Gunther a good scratching behind the ears. He wagged his tail and whined at me hungrily. "Where is everyone, huh? Where're Mom and Dad?"

Gunther jumped onto my bed and began whining at Connor, digging a cold nose into his skin.

Connor rolled over and pulled the blanket over his head, moaning as Gunther flopped down on top of him and began panting and grunting, eager to be taken out. "He's adorable, but please get him off me."

"You've got to get up," I said, hopping on the bed and gently shaking his shoulder. Gunther was drooling all over my sheets. "We can't be like this in here."

He turned and squinted up at me through sleepy eyes. "I thought you said this was *your* room and no one ever comes in here."

"They don't usually," I said. "But sometimes if my dad

is still drunk or comes home late, he'll stumble in here by mistake."

Connor crinkled his nose. "What if you're like, jacking off or something?"

"Shut up!" I said, and he laughed. "Why are you not wearing anything? I am. What the hell happened last night?"

He shrugged and smirked, not seeming to care either way. "Uh, you don't remember?" He sat up and kissed me, and I felt myself harden. "And you know I like to sleep in the nude."

"Seriously, though, get up," I said. "We have to leave."

I moved to stand, but he grabbed my shirt and pulled me back down on the bed. "What's your hurry? They're not here." He moved on top of me and kissed me again, his hands sliding down the small of my back.

"We can't," I heard myself say, but I was losing sight of the goal and the will to care. Gunther whined loudly. "I have to walk him. Get dressed." I resisted and pulled away from his warmth, throwing his clothes that were all over the ground at him and grabbing Gunther by the collar. "Come on, buddy, let's go out."

I was surprised to bump into Mom right outside my door. She was dressed in her tattered bathrobe and chewing a dry piece of toast. Her hair was tied up in a bun and held together with chopsticks. The kind from the fucking restaurants.

So much for the blueberry muffins and the plum-colored pantsuit.

"Oh hey, honey!" she said. "If you're hungry, I can make you something. I went out and got…well, *hello* there, Connor."

To my horror, Connor was standing there shirtless outside of my room—but wearing shorts, thank God—leaning against the doorframe and smiling at Mom like this was just an ordinary fucking day at the Burns household.

"Hey, Ellie," he said. "You look particularly lovely this morning."

"Well thank you, honey," she said, adjusting her chopsticks with a titter. *Gross.* "Anyway, if you boys are hungry I can whip up some pancakes. I just bought this great new mix at the Shop N' Save."

"That sounds great," said Connor. I wanted to run back into my room, pull the covers over my head and never come back out.

After Mom made her way downstairs, Connor leaned in to kiss me, but I stiffened at his touch.

"What?" he said. "What's your problem now, Jack?"

"Seriously? You can't at least put on a shirt in front of my mother?" I heard myself snap at him. I went back into my room and started rummaging through my drawers for something he could wear. "Where's your shirt?"

He tossed it at me. "There. It's right fucking there. I thought you had to take your dog for a walk."

Mom called from downstairs, asking if we wanted blueberries in our pancakes.

"Your mom is so cute," he said.

I wanted to talk to him, to explain why I was acting like such an asshole, but all the frustration that had been mounting inside me was making it hard to think straight, let alone speak. What if Dad had been here instead of Mom? What if he'd seen—or God forbid—*heard* us together last night in my room?

I really had to be more careful. Dad might've been at least a little suspicious after that comment I'd made about going off to "fuck" that loser buddy of mine. At the time, he'd looked at me like I was just being a smartass, trying to rile him up, and hadn't said anything more on the subject. But I couldn't risk it. We couldn't stay at my place anymore.

"Jack?" Connor said. "Talk to me. Please."

He walked over and put his hands on my shoulders, squeezing them. "Dude, it's fine, your Mom fucking *knows.* You know she knows. Come on, I'm here shirtless in your house in the morning; we're always out together. We sleep in the same bedroom. Do you really think she's that dumb?"

I shrugged him off me. "I got to walk Gunther," I mumbled. I needed to get outside, needed to get some air and get away from everyone.

39

Something was up with Jess. I'd seen her trailing the halls by herself lately, head down, music leaking from her headphones as other kids pushed past her. Once I tried to talk to her, tried calling her name, but she kept on walking like she hadn't heard me and let herself be swallowed up by the crowd.

In Government, we had a sub. He put on an old *Schoolhouse Rock!* tape and dozed off at his desk, a thin line of drool collecting on his chin. Most of the kids were on their phones or just dicking around quietly, but Valerie Baker's voice penetrated the room.

"Skye Russo is ditching her as fast as those dark roots are coming back in," she said with a laugh, using her little hand mirror as she swiped on clumpy mascara.

"I always thought she looked tacky as a blonde," said Asha Yardley, and the other girls nodded in agreement.

I usually tuned them out, their dull chatter white noise to my ears, but this time they were talking about Jess. My Jess. My palms got hot and I fought the urge to speak. *It'll just make it worse*, I told myself.

"I mean, I guess hanging out with Skye does have its advantages…" said Katie Oh.

"Yeah," Valerie Baker cut in. "If you like giving hand-jobs to seniors in exchange for designer purses and maybe a prom invite."

"And maybe, just maybe, breakfast at Denny's the morning after," Asha added. Valerie laughed so hard she almost poked herself in the eye with her mascara and grinned at her friend in approval.

"If she's anything like her big sister, homegirl's gonna be giving much more than hand-jobs," said Katie.

"Do you all ever talk about anything other than how superior you are to everyone else?" I snapped.

Katie's mouth opened and closed. Asha turned red and stared at her desk. Valerie put down her mascara and sized me up.

"I'm sorry," she said. "I don't remember inviting you in on this conversation, *Jack*."

"I'm pretty sure you invited everyone in the room, you've been talking so loud," I said, surprising myself. It felt good to speak up, to tell someone off in this dump for once. "Lay off Jess. None of you are saints, and if you possessed the smallest shred of empathy, you'd see she's going through a lot right now."

Asha and Katie looked to Valerie, who was now applying sparkly purple eye shadow to her lids, studying her face in her mirror like I wasn't there.

Valerie lowered her voice. "You would know about her rough times, Jack. You *were* the one getting all rape-y with her on the couch at Skye's party, weren't you?"

Katie gasped. Asha covered her hand with her mouth. A few kids looked over at us.

I grabbed my backpack and stormed out of the room, slamming the door on my way out. I kicked a locker hard, and the lock clanked and rattled against the metal. I needed a joint. A huge hit off a bong. I headed off to the courtyard and lit up under the big sycamore tree.

I realized I was shaking.

I tried writing Jess a note. I crumpled it up and tossed it out. I tried writing an email, but my hands fumbled all over the keyboard and nothing came out right. I thought about calling her, but no, she'd said she needed space. I would honor that space.

Still, I had to at least check to see if she was alright. We were still friends, weren't we? I sent her a quick text message: *You okay? I'm here if you want to talk.* My heart picked up as three little dots appeared below my text message. She was typing something. She was actually going to tell me! But then they vanished, and nothing.

I shoved my phone back into my pocket and went to my next class, trying to block it all out. If she didn't need me, she didn't need me.

Then, later, right before school was about to let out,

I spotted them: Connor and Jess, huddled together in a corner of the science wing. He leaned in close to her and whispered something to her, and my heart thumped so hard I could hear my pulse in my ears. Was he telling her about us? Jess bit her lip and stared down at the floor, and Connor moved in to give her a one-armed hug. She hugged him back.

When he walked towards me down the hall, I grabbed his arm and he gasped in surprised.

"Oh! Sorry, you startled me," he said.

"I saw you talking to Jess. What was that about?"

He was looking around all distracted, but he just shrugged, forced a smile. "Oh. Nothing. She just needed help with something. Some class thing."

"You weren't like, talking about me, were you?"

He laughed and quickly kissed me under my jaw, my favorite spot to be kissed. The hall was empty by now, but it still made me freeze, watching and waiting for someone to walk by and see. "You're all we ever talk about," he teased, but I moved away from him.

"Wait, so you've talked to her before? You guys talk in general?"

He gave me this look like I was losing my mind. "Of course. We have classes together. Is that a problem?" He sounded annoyed, maybe mad.

"No, forget it," I said. "I'm just worried about her. It seems like something's really bothering her lately."

He chewed at his lip. "Yeah. Well. If there is, she'll tell you when she's ready, you know?"

I swallowed down the questions I desperately wanted to ask. He wasn't telling me something. That was obvious.

But I didn't want him to be mad at me, or keep looking at me like that. I just wanted to go back to his house and watch movies and smoke, and for everything to be easy between us. I didn't want to think about Jess.

I didn't really want to think, period.

Still, as I followed him to his locker to get his skateboard, I tried again. One last time. I opened my messages and sent her one.

If you need anything, you know I'm here.

40

The anonymous phone calls on my cell started not long after.

They were all from numbers I didn't know. Each time I answered, all I would hear was heaving breathing, then something whispered I couldn't make out. At first, I blew it off as a prank, but after about a dozen or so, I started getting nervous, started yelling at the person on the other line to quit being a pussy and reveal themselves.

Sometimes they came with text messages, cryptic—not even whole words—but creepy. I'd block the number, but hours later, a different one would call me.

"They must be using some ID spoofing app," Connor reasoned. "It's probably just Toby and the Rudoys fucking with you. Keep blocking them and ignoring them."

Connor and I were standing outside of the school after the last class, sharing a cigarette. More like, I was chain-smoking and he could barely get a puff in.

"You need to slow down, babe," he said gently. I stiffened at the word. There were kids all around us, within earshot. What if they heard us? What if the Rudoy brothers had walked by that very second?

"Don't," I snapped. "Don't say that out in the open."

Even I knew I was acting weird, but I couldn't stop. It was like something or someone had taken over my body, and I was running on pure adrenaline. I leaned against my bike, fidgeting with the handles, pretending to check the air in the tires so I wouldn't have to look at him.

"Is this about those fucking phone calls?" Connor asked. "Jesus, Jack, just ask Toby about it. Demand him to fess up. If you don't, I will."

"No!" I said. "Don't say anything."

"Why not? What is up with you lately?" He put a hand on my shoulder, but I shrugged it off.

"I don't want to talk about it," I said. "Let's just go to your place."

He stood in front of me, blocking my bike as I tried to pedal off. "No," he said. "First of all, you're in a terrible mood, and you won't tell me why. Second, we do that every time, and it's starting to feel like we're fugitives." He gestured to the other kids standing around, smoking, laughing, chatting. Freshmen, athletes, artsy kids, theater kids, kids in gangs, kids who didn't really belong anywhere but still managed to somehow avoid being harassed by a vicious ghost on the phone. Carefree and easy-going and *la-dee-da* kids. And there was Skye Russo, twirling her hair with manicured fingers and flirting with some senior guy. In that moment, I hated them all.

And I hated Connor standing in my path, blocking me from moving. "Get out of the way, Connor."

"No," he said.

My phone bleeped. I reached reluctantly into my pocket, praying it was Mom or even Toby, but no. It was anonymous, as usual, some area code I didn't recognize.

RWILWEWY.

Riley was all I could see. It was like someone had mainlined adrenaline into my heart. I needed to pedal out of there, get out of there fast, but Connor was still in my way.

"What is it?" he asked, as if he didn't already know.

"Move!" I yelled, and some kids turned to stare at us. I rammed my bike so hard into his legs he was forced to jump to the side. I caught a glimpse of the look of shock and hurt on his face, but barely had time to register it. I had to get home, and I had to get home fast. That was all I knew.

I biked down the freeway, the sun beating down on me. Soon I was drenched with sweat. It felt like the temperature had turned up one hundred degrees. I rode past the crude billboards, the strip malls coated in garish colors, minivans and SUVs roasting in their gummy lots. Everything was loud—a big, muddled mess.

By the time I made it home, my legs hurt so badly I could barely walk to the front door. I kicked my bike and didn't bother locking it up in the garage. I didn't care anymore. Then I pulled my phone out of my pocket.

There was a text, but it was from Connor. It wasn't an accusation, or an angry message, or even a plea. It was just a heart, and in that moment, it was all I needed to calm down and root myself.

I tried. I really tried. But my head wouldn't stop spinning. My heart wouldn't stop racing.

And no matter how many times I blocked the numbers, the texts kept coming.

RWILWEWY.

RWILWEWY.

And each time, my stomach dropped. I shut off my phone.

41

He kissed my neck and I pulled away. It had been like this all day in school, him sneaking in sweet little gestures and trying to be close to me in math class, and me being the coward that I was. I wanted to kiss him back more than anything, to wrap my arms around him and let the whole school see us, but something always stopped me cold. Maybe it was the way that the Rudoy brothers or Toby would always sneer at us in the halls, and the way certain people were starting to whisper and laugh. It was like suddenly I heard and felt and saw everything, and everyone was always talking about me. Every conversation. Every passed note in class. I was paranoid, and I'd sit through class with my leg jiggling and my palms sweating and my stomach in knots.

I turned off my phone and started avoiding Connor in the hallways. It's not that I didn't want to see him. Not exactly. But he didn't understand. And I couldn't explain why I was so damn scared. Maybe it was that I knew deep down that I wasn't man enough for him, that I didn't really deserve him or any of this.

"What is it?" he asked. We were sequestered in the bathroom in the science wing during an assembly. "Why do you keep avoiding me? I know you are. You pretend like you don't see me or know me. But then when we go back to my house, or somewhere else, you're a totally different person." I could hear the edge in his voice and see the mix of anger and hurt in his eyes. It was just us in that dirty bathroom, my nerves on edge, listening, waiting for someone to come in...to see us. To see me. To see us.

"Jack," he said. "Let me inside your head for once."

"I can't," I mumbled. I turned from him and went to the sink, pressing my face against the glass of the mirror. He reached out to touch my shoulder, and I didn't mean to, but I pulled away.

I instantly regretted it. We were standing on the precipice of something, and I was pushing us over the edge.

He was silent for a moment, and then he spoke.

"You know, Jack, I've tried. I've really tried. This has been going on since I first met you."

I went somewhere deep inside myself. I knew this would come...I'd known it all along.

I'd willed it into existence.

"But now you're farther away from me than ever. I understand you're scared, and not just of those phone calls. I get that. Trust me, if anyone knows fear, it's me. But if this is going to work, if we're going to...I just can't keep hiding out like this, like some frightened fucking animal."

When I didn't answer, he went on. "You know how I feel about this place, about the assholes that go here. Well *fuck them all.* Seriously, *fuck them.* Jack, come on, look at me. You matter more to me than these shitty people with their heads so far up their own asses they can't breathe or think of anyone but themselves or anything but their own ignorant bullshit. Jack. Answer me!"

A thousand words were caught in my throat, swimming through my mind, but I couldn't speak.

I heard him leave then, heard the door swing shut, the sound echoing into the cold chamber of everything I was making myself lose.

42

The rattlesnake was enormous, monstrous.

Its long, meaty body writhed in pain in the giant oven that was slowly burning it to death. Someone tapped me on the shoulder and handed me a spoon. I'd have to eat it when it was done cooking.

I woke up gasping for air. My lungs on fire. Mom was there, rubbing my back. "You're alright," she said soothingly. "It was just a nightmare."

My sheets were sticky with sweat. I was shaking, terrified, the horror and the panic rising in me from some primal place. My teeth chattered as she put a cool hand to my forehead and rubbed my shoulders.

"It's okay, baby," she said. "Everything's alright now."

I let her tuck me back in, let her bring me water and feel my forehead again, gauging my temperature. Soon the chills ceased and I stopped shaking, the heaviness setting in as I settled back down. I could see her wrinkles in the darkness, the familiar shape of her face, all the lines and creases, the way her hair fell forward down her shoulders.

"Mom," I whispered. "Something bad is going to happen." It was something I used to say when I was little, when I would wake from a bad dream, a long series of night terrors I used to get when I was nine or ten.

She dutifully said her lines.

"No, no," she said, her voice a balm. "Everything is going to be just fine. When you wake up in the morning, everything will be better."

For the first time in a while, I felt love for her. Deep, endless rivers of love, warming me as I fell back into a stone-cold sleep.

In the morning, I fished through my drawers, finally settling on one of my favorite shirts, a white graphic tee. On the front was a black-and-white photo of a handsome young James Dean, smoking a thin cigarette. I spiked my hair up in the front, checking myself out in the mirror. I looked good. *I look good. I feel good,* I told myself.

It was warm and sunny that day, a cool breeze following me as I biked the two miles to school. Today would be different, it would be better. No one would try me today.

Things were going well until second period, when I went to my locker.

Carved into the metal was the letter "F", revealing the cold gray steel underneath the sickly orange paint. It'd been done with a key or a knife, something that could allow for a quick and easy cut.

I scouted the hallways for someone watching me, someone waiting for my reaction. But there was no one there that I knew, just pools of freshmen floating along aimlessly, happily oblivious.

I breathed deeply, forced myself to relax. *They can't hurt you*, I told myself. *They're just trying to rattle you.*

I opened my locker.

Inside was a thick piece of rope fashioned into what looked like a noose. A pink sticky note had been stuck to it, along with the words in barely eligible writing: *No one would miss you.* And beside it, a badly drawn cartoon of Riley Adams, naked and covered in black scribbles.

I slammed the locker door so hard it rattled.

I felt myself getting hot all over, and suddenly it was hard to breathe. Things were tunneling away from my vision, the ground pulling me underneath.

There were voices, a security guard snapping for me to move along, someone asking if I was okay. We were moving. Things were fuzzy, blurry. In my mind's eye, I was in the backyard, running away from Daddy, heart racing, cold adrenaline sweating off me. I had to move quickly or the monster would catch me. Everything was very bright.

I didn't come to until someone laid me down on my back. I stared up at the ugly school ceiling, white with black spots.

The school nurse was sitting on the edge of the sick bed, taking my pulse with two fingers. She had a placid, small smile on her face, a knowing look that made me feel calm.

"What happened?" I asked.

"I'm not too sure, hon. It looks like you may have had a panic attack. Have you experienced anything like this before?"

I shook my head. "No, I don't know. Maybe."

She helped me sit up. "Slowly, slowly. There you go." She handed me a Dixie cup filled with water. I gulped it down and immediately wanted more. Why did they make these things so small?

"You're okay, now," she said gently, her voice like warm milk. But I didn't feel okay.

"Do you want me to call your parents and have them pick you up?"

"No, no. I'm fine."

"I just need to see your student I.D., get some stuff logged into the system, and then you can head back to class if you're feeling up to it."

I shook my head. The dizzy feeling was coming back full throttle. "Please, can we just keep this between us?" I said. "I don't want this in the system. I don't want my parents knowing. I don't want anyone to know. Look, I know it's your job and all, but I'm fine, really. I don't want anyone worrying about me. Can we just…act like this didn't happen?"

She wiped her glasses on his shirt and studied me closely. "What's your name?"

"Jack," I said. "Burns."

"Jack, here's what I'm going to do. I'm going to write an excuse for you that says you were sick that you can give to your teacher, and I'll log this into the system as a stomach-related issue. I do think you should call your mom or dad and have them come pick you up early. I'll be more than happy to arrange that, and I won't tell them what happened."

"I think I'll go back to class," I said, forcing myself to smile.

She sighed and shook her head, writing up the note, but before she relinquished it to me she said: "Listen Jack, I'm only a school nurse, and this is just a suggestion, but if you feel this overwhelmed a lot, I would recommend seeing a counselor. You know, someone you can talk to besides Mom and Dad."

"Sure," I said, taking the note, forcing another smile. "Thanks."

I left the nurse's office, crumpling the note in my fist. I got the pink sticky note, cartoon, and rope from my locker, shoved them in my bag, and went outside to unlock my bike from the rack.

When I got home the house was quiet except for Gunther curled up against the wall with his legs splayed out, snoring loudly. It was weird that Mom wasn't there eating a bag of donuts or watching bad TV, but I didn't question it.

I let Gunther into the yard and sat in the grass. First, I burned the rope, watching it smolder and disintegrate into the ground until I needed to stomp out the flames. Then I burned the pink sticky note and the cartoon, watching the smoke curl and rise into the blue sky. I rolled a joint and laid back into the soft grass and smoked until my eyes watered and all the thoughts left my head.

43

I finally switched my phone back on.

For the past few days, I'd been avoiding Connor for

real. I'd kept my phone off, mostly to avoid the texts and calls, but also having to avoid the circle we kept going around and around in, the things he wanted from me that I couldn't give him.

No new messages. Nothing more from the creeps harassing me. And…nothing from Connor.

I was kind of relieved. We wouldn't have to fight about it again—about being out and proud for everyone at school—or whatever it was he wanted us to do.

But it also made me kind of nauseous, like maybe this time he was done with me for real.

The hands on the clock in English class slowed to a crawl. My teacher's voice became a low, dull buzzing in my ears. All I could think about was Connor, how I'd fucked things up with him, how I wanted to apologize. But there was nothing more I could say. My heart ached. My head ached. And fucking Toby was watching me all class period. Whenever I met his gaze, he'd turn around again, act like he wasn't looking. I thought I must've been hallucinating from paranoia.

The bell rang, and to my surprise he stepped in front of me before I could leave the room. "Get lunch with me and Max?" he asked. His eyes were all friendly, his smile reassuring.

Maybe I'd been imagining it all. Maybe it wasn't Toby who'd been sending me all those messages. Maybe he'd just been fucking around.

"Uh, maybe?" I said.

His smile dropped a little. "You have other plans?"

I could only shrug. I guess I didn't.

I searched Toby's eyes for a sign of reassurance. A sign

that things between us were alright. "Yeah. Sure, I guess." Maybe he wanted to apologize to me in person about being such a dick for so long. Toby had never been good at conversation, about being direct with how he felt. I should at least give him a chance.

"Cool. Max is picking up some sandwiches. We're meeting at the usual spot. You know, the one we used to go to. You do remember *that*, right?"

Of course I remembered. It was the spot by the big, fat palm trees in the courtyard. We used to eat there every day, two of us waiting while one of us made a fast-food run.

I opened my mouth to answer him when my phone *dinged.*

A new message.

My face lit up immediately. I couldn't help it. It was from Connor, asking where I'd been. He was annoyed, obviously, but this was a sign. A sign that he wasn't completely done with me, that he still cared after all. I let out a breath of relief.

But when I looked back up at Toby, he wasn't smiling anymore. "Who is that?" he asked, trying to get a look at my screen. "Who texted you?"

"Huh?"

Ding. Another message: *I miss you so much.*

I could've melted right into the floor. I texted back quickly: *Meet me in the courtyard.*

"Who is that?" Toby moved again to look.

Ding.

Okay.

Ding.

I love you.

"Cut it out, Toby!"

And even though I'd pulled my phone away, I knew that this time, Toby had seen it—the very last message—because his face had lost all of its color.

My throat was so dry. *He knows for sure now. He knows.*

When he spoke, his voice was eerily calm, his eyes void of any emotion. "Just show me, Jack," he said. "Show me what it says." He moved to grab my phone from me, but I pulled away, accidentally bumping into a girl trying to leave. She yelped in pain and glared at me on her way out the door.

"I'm so sorry!" I said. "Jesus, Toby, what the hell is your problem?"

"I just want to see who texted you," he said. Like it was no big deal. Like this was a perfectly reasonable thing for him to be asking me.

"What? Why? It's none of your business. What is up with you lately?"

"Gentlemen," Mrs. Flores said. "I'm going to have to ask you to stop blocking the doorway."

"Fine," Toby said, in that creepy, calm voice. "Forget it, Jack. Let's just go to lunch."

I followed him to our old spot in silence, my temples throbbing with pain. Toby glanced around for security guards, then lit a cigarette. I watched a cloud of smoke escape his lips and turn into a sneer. We didn't speak for what felt like forever. My leg was jiggling again, my palms dripping with sweat. The laughing and chatting around us warped into a muffled, muted, white stream of noise. It was just us in this bubble now, and it was only a matter of time until it burst.

"Yo, did you want bacon, Toby?" Max's cheerful greeting popped a tiny hole in the bubble, letting in some breathable air. He tossed the paper bags at us and plopped down beside me.

Toby just grunted and tore into his, barely bothering with the aluminum wrapping. I stared at mine until Max nudged me with his elbow.

"You gonna eat that?" he asked me, his mouth full of food. I searched his eyes for some kind of intent, some knowing, but they were pure and clear.

I shrugged and pushed it aside. "Not hungry," I said. My stomach growled in quiet protest.

"*Already got his mouth full.*" I heard it, I swear, a murmur audible only to me. Toby was wolfing down his sandwich, staring out across the courtyard as if I didn't exist.

I took a deep breath, trying to be calm, even as my chest tightened and searing chills ran through my body.

"What was that?" I asked.

Max said something, but I couldn't hear him. I was focused only on Toby, who hadn't even moved his head.

"Speak up, Toby. What the fuck did you just say?" The anger was rising inside me, snapping my vocal chords into action.

He swallowed and met my gaze. "You heard me."

"Say it again, you pussy."

"What are you guys talking about?" Max asked. He sounded scared.

"Shut the fuck up, Max," Toby spat, throwing a wrapper in his direction. He leaned closer to me, and I could smell the hot sauce on his breath. "I said, you deaf little shit, it's no wonder you ain't hungry, 'cause you already got a mouthful of dick."

My stomach corkscrewed. I tried to speak, but my mouth was shut with wire and tasted like metal.

He smirked and pulled away from me, satisfied for now. The noise around us was beginning to come back into focus, everything inside me a dull haze. I stood up to leave.

"Jack?" Max's voice rose tentatively, dumbfounded no doubt.

I turned my back on them and walked away, hearing Toby tell Max, "Don't bother with him. Dude, it's true. I know it's true now, about both of them. I fucking saw something just now. And you ain't gonna *believe* this shit, Max, what that little bitch has been texting him."

Connor. He was calling Connor a little bitch. Through the fog in my brain I pieced it together, and then I walked back to them, grabbed Toby's shirt collar, and yanked his scrawny ass off the ground.

A group of students were beginning to form around us, gravitating to the mounting tension that promised a fight.

"Don't you ever fucking talk about him," I heard myself say. We were so close we could hear each other breathing.

And then he said it slowly, the cruel word dipped in poison that rolled off his tongue like venom. "What are you gonna do, faggot?"

Max stood behind him dumbly.

Then I felt hands around my waist, familiar hands, pulling me aside and out of the way. I smelled cologne and cigarette smoke and a hint of coconut shampoo.

Connor raised his fist and punched Toby dead in the nose.

He hit the ground hard, blood pouring down his face. Someone screamed. Now the group of kids had circled around us, chanting shit about a fight, *beat his ass, beat his ass!* Max rushed to Toby's side, asking him again and again if he was okay while Toby moaned pitifully.

There was a flurry of hands, movement, yells of "Let's go!" and "Move out of the way!" Security surrounded us, pulling Connor's hands behind his back. One of the guards pushed my shoulder and moved me along through a stream of curious faces, rows of kids lined up to get a glimpse of the action, some of them laughing.

We were herded back inside and into the administrative office, where I sat in a metal folding chair on the other side of the room from Connor, who had two guards on each side of him. I heard grave voices, something about the police being called.

I felt words in my throat, things caught in my chest I wanted to say, but I couldn't speak. I heard the buzz of walkie-talkies, saw the cops come in and talk to the guards, then put handcuffs around Connor's wrists. "You are under arrest. You have the right to remain silent. Anything you say or do may be used against you in a court of law..." His jaw was clenched tight, but he stared ahead, cooperating coolly, quietly defiant. His eyes caught mine for a moment before someone stepped in front of me, blocking him from my line of sight.

An administrator gestured for me to get up. I craned my neck but I couldn't see him as they led him out the door. "Come on, son," the man said. He led me down the hall in the direction of the principal's office.

44

"I'm in the middle of a meeting," Principal Oliver said gently. "Go wait outside, please."

To my surprise, Jess was at the door, peering in, her face flushed and sweaty. A secretary was clucking at her from behind.

"I'm sorry, sir, she just barged on in." The secretary had one manicured hand pressed against the door, trying to prevent Jess from opening it any further.

But Jess was relentless. "Is Jack in there?" She craned her neck around and broke into a sad smile when she saw me. "Jack!"

I wanted the ugly green carpet to swallow me up. I wanted to disappear forever. I looked down at my dirty sneakers.

"Please, Miss Velez," Principal Oliver said. "I can speak with you when I'm finished."

"He didn't do anything wrong," Jess said. "Toby called him a f—a name. A really terrible name. Everyone heard it. Connor was just defending him."

I thought about swimming out into the ocean so far that the current pulled me under. I thought about how long it would take to hitchhike to Santa Cruz.

"Tell him, Jack! Tell him what he said to you! Isn't there a policy against hate speech in this state? How can you let that go unpunished?"

Principal Oliver sighed like one might when a toddler is causing a ruckus.

"Come inside," he said, motioning for her to sit. "I'll

give you five minutes to say your peace, and then I need to speak to Mr. Burns." The secretary scoffed and left us there, the door shutting with a bang.

Principal Oliver really was doing his best, all things considered. He was in his mid-forties, but he looked like he was pushing sixty—white whiskers, a deeply receding hairline. He probably didn't sleep or get out much. I wondered if he ever went home at night and thought about just ending it all.

He put his palms up, as if asking us what we wanted him to do. "As I was just explaining to Mr. Burns, assault is prohibited at this school, and that includes verbal *and* physical. There is no excuse for hitting someone in the face, and as a school we will not tolerate that behavior. This has been quite a problem this year, as I'm sure you've noticed, and we are cracking down on it."

"But—"

"Jessica, please let me finish. As I said, there is no excuse for what happened today. A student of mine was injured, and this was not the first time Mr. Orellana has engaged in unacceptable behaviors on this campus. That being said, that discussion does not concern either of you. And neither of you are in trouble right now. I need to get a clear timeline of what happened. Is what Jessica said true, Jack? Did Toby provoke you?"

I blinked at him. What did he want me to say? Did he really want me to repeat the word, to reveal why Connor had reacted the way he did?

"I was a witness," Jess said.

Principal Oliver nodded. "Alright. But I'd like to hear from Jack now."

I shrugged.

"Jack? Is there anything you'd like to say?" Principal Oliver pressed.

Jess rose from her seat. "Jack! If you won't tell him, I will!"

I finally met her frantic eyes. "Sit down, Jess," I said, and it came out meaner than I'd intended. "Just stay out of this."

"Please Jack," she pleaded. "I might be mad at you, but you're my best friend. I can help. I love you."

Part of me ached for her, even after all of this time apart. It was like a reflex. I wanted to reach out and hug her, and reassure her, and wipe the smudged eyeliner from her cheek and tell her that it was going to be fine. But I didn't have it in me anymore. I was tired, so damn tired.

So I turned to Principal Oliver and said: "I'm not comfortable discussing this right now. I'm sorry." Without waiting for a reply, I swung my backpack over my shoulder, strode out of the room, and left her there.

45

The living room was wrecked. The stench of beer was everywhere, infusing the room with its sickly, sour odor. Dad sat in his La-Z-Boy amid a smashed lamp, broken bottles, torn papers, and documents. The coffee table was overturned. The remains of the ceramic pig I had painted for Mom for her thirty-fourth birthday lay in ruins in a corner. I spotted a pink snout and a hoof.

Mom wasn't here. I knew that before I walked in. Her car had vanished from its customary spot next to the sycamore. And he just sat there, bloated and bleary-eyed in his stained white t-shirt and acid-washed jeans, head in his hands. Maybe he was expecting her to come home once she'd cooled off or expecting me to stay here and clean up the mess he'd made, once again.

"Where's Mom?" I demanded.

Dad stared down at a beer stain on the carpet. "She's gone."

"Where, Dad? I asked where!"

"She's staying at the Castle Motel for a while."

"Oh, that's just *fucking* great!" I threw my backpack to the floor, knocking over another bottle. Fuck it. Fuck him. "Did you hit her, huh? Did you threaten to? You broke all this shit, didn't you?" I kicked at the smashed ceramic pig snout. Gunther barked at me from across the room.

"She broke it all, son," Dad said quietly to the floor.

"Oh bull*shit*, Dad!" I could feel it, all of the rage and frustration I'd been bottling up for weeks. It was spilling out of me now, leaking all over the carpet, joining the beer and the broken shards of glass. "You made her run away, didn't you? She's always been scared of you! You don't think I remember all those times you got drunk and tore up the fucking house? You don't think I remember the last time she left you, when she took me with her so you wouldn't kill me?"

He was staring at me now with wide, bloodshot eyes, shaking his head. "No, Jack. That's not what happened."

"You're such a liar! You don't think I get it? She left

behind everything for you! She left law school for you, to stay home and be your fucking maid!"

"She left law school because she was sick, Jack," he said. "Your mother is very sick."

"No, *you're* sick! You're a drunk."

"I know I'm a drunk."

"And you made her leave."

He inhaled a deep, ragged breath. "I didn't make her leave. She chose to leave. And she wanted to take you with her again. Throw you and your things in her car in the middle of the night and drive away somewhere where I couldn't find you, to punish me. Just like she did when you were four."

Now it was me shaking my head. "No, that can't be true. She was afraid of you."

"I may be a drunk and I may get too angry, but I'm not the one who breaks things. She wanted to take you away from me, not just to punish me. To scare me. It worked the first time. I wouldn't let it happen a second time. I promised myself that. I told her that she had a choice. Either get help, or get out of this house."

Gunther whined from his spot in corner, all curled up with his head down. My throat tightened. Pain sliced through my chest. I couldn't do this. I couldn't be here another second.

"Fuck this shit," I said. I grabbed my backpack off the floor and headed for the door.

"Where are you going?" he asked. He sounded so old, so tired and broken.

"I don't know, okay? But I can't be here! Not with you. Not while you're still lying to me."

"Jesus, Jack. At least take some money." He stood and reached into his pocket, offering me a $50 bill. It gave me pause. We were broke. That was probably as much as he'd made in tips last night. I wanted to take it so bad, to accept it, but accepting felt like giving in.

"I don't want your money," I mumbled.

"You need something. What are you even going to do, Jack?"

"I'll figure it out." I stood like that for a moment, watching him, as if daring him to stop me.

He didn't move.

I turned and left him there, slamming the door, running as fast as I could from that awful fucking house that I hated loving. I didn't stop until I was back at the alley behind my grandfather's old building, where he'd died and left me here with all of the broken pieces. I slammed my fist against the cheap siding again and again and again, then crumpled to the ground and cried like I'd never cried before.

46

I should've taken the fucking $50 bill.

I didn't have much money on me. Maybe enough for a night or two at a motel and a sandwich. Maybe I could stay with Mom.

But the farther I got from my house and my dad, the more all of those things he'd said felt less and less like lies. There could be truth in it. Mom was unstable. I knew that. She had issues. But would she really kidnap me? Break everything in her own house, even things I'd made for her? She'd cried when I'd given her that stupid ceramic pig.

No, it couldn't be the whole truth. I wouldn't let it be the truth.

I continued down San Juan Boulevard, feeling lost and dazed among the evening crowd. The sunlight was weakening, and everything would be dark and creepy soon.

I thought about going to Jess's house. Maybe her dad would let me crash on the couch or sleep in her old room. I remembered it vividly, its mint green walls striped with hot pink, its cushy furniture and big comfy bed. I'd let her paint my toenails once, the day her air conditioning was broken and we watched a cheesy horror flick on DVD in our underwear. I even let her practice doing eyeliner on me, even though she poked me in the eye a few times. I didn't care. She was the most real friend I ever had.

I stopped to take a break, setting my bag down a moment to rest my aching shoulders. I sent her a quick text: *Hey, can I come over?* And I sat on the ground and leaned against the wall of the 7-11. Then I saw him walk out.

It was the short little man with the twitching eye, the one who'd sold knives on a baby blanket. His scrunched face was dark with sunburn, his clothes tattered and dirty. He hobbled forward and crouched down next to me. His odor was strong, earthy but not unclean.

"Got any spare change?" he asked me. I heard the thickness in his accent, something South American.

I shook my head. The sun made its final descent as everything grew dark. People passed us without even so much as a second look. I wondered what it was like to live on the streets, to watch people pass by with their shopping bags full of good food that they'd take back to their warm and safe homes, where they'd resume their normal lives full of endless trivialities that seemed like luxuries to those who had nothing. I wondered what it was like to feel like your life was empty and meaningless, a sad fading light that no one noticed was fading.

He put something in front of my face that startled me. A photo of a rattlesnake, printed out in black and white on computer paper. I turned to look at him and saw he had a stack of them and was trying to hand them out to people nearby.

"What is this?" I asked.

He held it closer to me, urgently. "You need to be careful. This is important," he said. "It'll explain everything." I didn't look at him, didn't want to see that big twitching eye. I shook my head.

"Take it," he hissed, shoving it into my hands.

"I have to go," I said.

"You have to listen to me," he said, pointing to the snake. His fingernails were caked with dirt and what looked like blood. "They're coming. It will come after you too."

"What are you doing out here?"

The familiar voice made me look up. It was Alvaro, Connor's uncle, holding a six-pack in one hand and adjusting a pair of Ray Bans with the other.

"I thought it was you," he said. "You okay? You need a ride?"

I opened my mouth but nothing came out. "Come on," he said softly, putting a hand on my shoulder. "You shouldn't be here by yourself this late."

He tossed my bag into the backseat of his Jeep as I slid

inside. "Fasten your seatbelt," he told me. I followed his order listlessly, letting my head sink into the soft leather as we pulled away from the curb. I watched the twitchy-eyed man stare as we drove until he was out of sight.

"You know anything about what happened at school today? About the fight?" he asked.

I shrugged.

"You must know something. Must have heard something, at least."

"Where's Connor?" I asked.

"He's at the police station, in a holding cell. He can spend the night in there," he said. "I'll get him out tomorrow. He has to learn that's not the way to handle things, punching people in the face."

"That's not fair," I said. "And it was my fault he hit him, anyway."

"Oh, so you *do* know what went down."

"Sort of," I said. "This guy I know was…saying something to me. Something really awful. And I guess Connor heard him and, well, you know." I mimed a kid getting punched in the face and tried to smile, but Alvaro didn't smile back. He just sighed this really deep, tired sigh. "I guess it was kind of my fault."

"Hey, look at me," Alvaro said. I did. His face was set in a stern frown. "Did you punch that kid? Did you break his nose? No? Then it wasn't your fault. You're not responsible for other people's actions, Jack."

"And as for fair," he continued. "You think the system's gonna go easy on a kid that looks like him? This isn't the first time, and I'll be damned if it's not the last. He is not gonna end up like his parents." He put his hand to his mouth and grimaced at some painful, private memory.

I was quiet for a moment, watching the crumbling roads dissolve into the freeway we'd merged onto, the endless landscape of pavement and steel and nothingness. "He's lucky to have you around," I said. My throat felt tight and I tried to swallow it down.

His face softened. "Hey, relax. Look at your fists. You don't need to be all worked up."

I realized I'd been holding onto something tight. I unfolded the picture of the snake that I'd crumpled into my hands.

It was an insurance advertisement. The guys around here got paid to hand these out. They handed them to everyone.

They meant nothing.

I watched where the snake had landed on the car floor. Oddly, I felt a pang of disappointment. Just a moment ago, this piece of paper had seemed so important to that man. Like he was really trying to tell me something, some secret meaning that would make sense of everything.

The eyes of the snake seemed to glower at me, vague and incomprehensible, the black and white image of the giant cobra so menacing on the clean white piece of paper.

I checked my phone. Nothing from Jess.

As we pulled up to Alvaro's house I could feel the exhaustion sinking in, slowly pulling me under. But I was glad to be here, where Connor lived, with his uncle whose every movement didn't leave my teeth on edge, didn't have me waiting for the next sharp word, the next big fight. He was calming. So was the slow, ticking sound of the wall clock, the gentle humming of the fridge. Everything in here was so smooth and clean and quiet. I sat down on a stool at the kitchen island while he sorted through his mail.

"You want some coffee? Tea?" he asked.

I shook my head.

"You must be hungry. How long were you out there by the 7-11 with that creepy guy?"

"Not long." I felt embarrassed, having run off like that. Where was I even trying to go? "My dad was drinking and saying all kinds of stuff, so I left."

Alvaro nodded and then reached into a cupboard, pulling a tube of Neosporin and a box of Band-Aids. "You mind if I take a look at those hands?"

I stared down at my bruised, beat-up knuckles. I hadn't even felt the pain after smashing my fist into that wall. "I think I'm okay."

"You mind if I take a look anyway?"

I shrugged and let him examine my hands, let him apply the Neosporin that burned like hell when it touched an open cut. "So, your dad's been drinking, huh?"

"It's his favorite pastime."

"And you just left home? Thought you'd go hang out at the Strip for the night? Hang out with the homeless guys and the hookers?"

I grinned. "Something like that."

"What about your mom? Does she live with you guys?"

I winced. "Sort of. I mean, yeah. But she went out for a while. I don't really know if she's coming back."

He tore open a Band-Aid. "I should call your dad, let him know you're staying here at a friend's and that you're okay. I feel like that's the responsible thing to do here, you know?"

He offered me the Band-Aid, and I took it and wrapped it around the cut on my finger. It didn't help the pain, but somehow it made things feel a little better. I gave him my home phone number and my dad's cell. And it was nice, letting an adult just take over for once.

I decided to ask for something in return, something that I'd been wanting so badly to know. Maybe if Connor wouldn't tell me, Alvaro would. "What happened exactly with Connor's parents?"

He sighed deeply. "They're addicts, Jack. Good, loving people taken by the terrible disease of addiction. They've been in prison for the past ten years, serving hard time for possession and trafficking."

"So, they're…criminals," I said, letting the word sink in.

"Yes, they're criminals. Listen Jack, I want you to have my number. May I?" I shrugged and handed him my phone, and he entered his digits. "If you ever need anything at all, or you find yourself wandering the streets again, please don't hesitate to call or text me. Anytime."

"Can't you just go get Connor now? All he did was punch some asshole. Is that really worth spending a night in jail over?"

"You have to understand, Jack. Connor's got…things he needs to deal with. Impulses. Dangerous ones. He does things that scare me. Reckless things. Sometimes I think he…" He cleared his throat and shook his head as if he'd said too much. But I needed to know.

"You think he what? Just tell me. He wouldn't be mad

if you told me." I didn't know if this was true, but I didn't care. I needed to understand.

Alvaro cleared his throat. "He's been through a lot. Things I can't even imagine. Sometimes I think he has some kind of a death wish."

I shut my eyes tight, trying to keep the room from tilting, trying hard to breathe. *In, out, in out.* If I just breathed, it would all be okay.

"You think he wants to die?" I asked. My voice sounded so small. The room—the kitchen, the house, the stool I was sitting on—it all felt so far away.

Alvaro's cell phone rang. We both jumped, and he looked relieved as he took the call and left the room, giving me a look that said we'd talk about it later.

But I knew we wouldn't. And that was okay. He'd already said enough.

47

The next morning, I listened to Alvaro's car pull into the garage, waiting for Connor like an anxious puppy. The door opened and there he was, looking dirty and tired but still impossibly beautiful in an old UCLA sweatshirt. After Alvaro squeezed past us, I hugged Connor, burying my face in the soft fabric.

"I need to shower," he mumbled into my neck.

"I don't care," I said.

He locked his arms around me, and I inhaled his familiar smell.

"I'm sorry," I said, my voice cracking pathetically. "I'm so sorry."

"Hey, it's okay," he said, rubbing my back. "Why are you sorry?"

He pulled away a little to look me in the eye, and then spotted my bruised, beat-up knuckles. "What happened?"

"Jack, you mind helping me with the groceries?" Alvaro asked, like he'd sensed I didn't want to answer.

"I'll be up in a minute," I said to Connor.

By the time I came upstairs, Connor was curled up under the covers, asleep. He looked so peaceful. I tried to lie down as quietly as possible, but the second my head touched a pillow his eyes snapped open.

"Hey," he said, looking happy to be awakened.

"I'm guessing you didn't sleep last night," I said.

He shook his head and pressed his face into the pillow, moaning. "Trust me man, you never want to end up in jail. I feel like shit."

I stripped down to my boxers and crawled under the sheets beside him. "Does he care?" I asked, tilting my head toward downstairs.

"No," he said. "He never comes in here. And he knows."

"About us?" I asked. The words were tangled deep in my throat, and saying them aloud felt like melting off the frost. "Did you tell him?"

Connor shrugged. "Not really, but…he just knows. You know?"

I thought of my mom. How she just knew. How she just saw me. It hurt so badly to think of her.

I inched closer to his chest, and he wrapped his arm around me, letting me huddle into the warmth of his body.

His breathing was starting to slow and deepen, and in spite of all the anger and anxiety coiled tight in me like a spring, I felt myself beginning to unravel.

"What happened to your hand?" he asked.

"Nothing," I said.

"Bullshit."

"Seriously, it's nothing."

"Jack—"

"Can we just lie here like this for a little while? And not talk?"

He was silent for a moment and then rolled over from me and defiantly went to sleep.

I lay there listening to him breathe, tracing *I love you, too,* on his skin with my fingertips.

48

I woke up to Connor bringing me coffee. It smelled good, gourmet. I reached for it gratefully.

I was groggy and dazed from the nap, the sun already starting to set, but my headache had receded to a dull pressure. Connor sat down on the bed and told me we needed to talk about something, something that couldn't wait.

"I lied to you the other day," he said. "About Jess and I talking in the hallways. It wasn't nothing. We were talking about…about Toby. About something that happened to her."

The coffee burned my tongue. "Why would you lie to me? What are you even talking about?"

"I'm sorry," he said. "I just didn't know how you'd react. I barely knew what to do myself when I heard it."

"Heard what?"

Connor sighed and lay down on the bed next to me, examining his nails. "She was crying in Spanish. Like, tears in her eyes and everything, head down on her desk, and she doesn't really have any friends in that class. And we talk sometimes, you know, about homework and assignments and stuff, and so—"

"Connor," I said, putting the mug down and inching closer to him. He never stumbled over his words like this. "You're making me really nervous. What is it?"

He pulled a joint from his pocket and lit up, exhaling a cloud of thick smoke that unraveled as it rose to the ceiling. "You're gonna need a hit or two of this."

I took a really long hit.

"I asked her if she was okay, if she wanted to talk, and she said sure, and we ended up talking for a few minutes after class. Well, mostly I just listened. She told me that something had happened with Toby, something really upsetting, and she felt like she couldn't trust anyone anymore. I could tell she could barely trust me, but she needed to tell me, you know? She needed to talk to someone.

"And I just nodded and waited for her to go on, and then she told me that she'd been at his house over the weekend, and they'd started making out or whatever, and then she'd told him she didn't like him like that. She didn't want it to be serious or whatever. And then he'd like… gotten really aggressive with her, started feeling her up, even though she was begging him to stop and was crying and really, really scared. And he kept trying to…you know.

Maybe he was trying to rape her, I don't know. She said he was holding her hands down so it was hard to move. But eventually she kicked him hard enough and got him off of her and got away and…shit, I don't know if I can tell you this. If I should. It's really personal, you know? But I haven't been able to stop thinking about it. And so I said, you know, Jess, maybe you should tell someone else. Like your mom or dad or something. I didn't know what else to do."

No, I thought. *No no no no no no.*

It was a good thing we were near his bathroom, because soon I was running to it and puking up hot coffee. It burned my esophagus on the way back up. Connor patted my back and made me finish the joint.

I was shaking and I couldn't stop. That was why she'd been so upset lately. Because of *Toby.* I wanted to hit something, someone, anyone. I wanted to find Toby and chop off his dick and feed it to him and hear him cry and beg and scream.

And it was my fault, too. I'd started all of this. If I hadn't touched her like that at the party, if we hadn't had that falling out, Toby never would have gone after her, and they probably never would've started talking or hanging out. And he probably never would've—

"I didn't know what to do," Connor said again. He sounded small and helpless, like he was about to start crying. "I wrestled with it for days, trying to think of what I'd want someone to do if it were me. I couldn't handle telling you. I know how much you love her. I just didn't know what to do."

"I'm going to kill him," I said. "I'm going to find Toby

wherever he is right now and beat his ass to death. No. I need to call her. I need to call her right now."

"Jack!" Connor said. "Oh God, I knew I shouldn't have told you."

"I'm glad you did." I reached for my phone and dialed Jess' number, and it rang, and rang, and rang, going straight to voicemail every time.

I left a message. "Hey, it's me. Connor told me about what happened with Toby. And it's okay if you're mad at him for telling me, and still mad at me, too, because honestly, I don't blame you. But I want you to know that I'm here for you. And if you don't want to talk to me, that's okay, too. I just hope you're alright. I'm sorry, Jess. I'm so, so sorry." I hung up and tossed the phone across the room.

Then I was sobbing. Deep, ugly, heaving sobs.

Connor wrapped his arms around me and let me just cry for a while, cry snot and tears into his pillow. It felt like I'd cried more in these last few days than I'd ever cried in my life. And then he asked me, gently: "What's one place around here that makes you feel really calm? It can be anywhere. Wherever it is, we'll go there. Right now."

49

Sunscreen smells like childhood, like sticky-fingered freedom. The burning sun and the coolness of the chemical water, so cerulean, the tinkling of the ice cream truck's Spanish folk tunes, a call to action for kids to beg their parents for spare change…

I remembered all of this as I sat there on the cracked concrete with Connor at the edge of the pool, our feet dipped in the shallow water. The freeway roared softly behind the towering bushes that enclosed the tail end of the community center. Crickets and road noise, the smell of gasoline mixed with chlorine, bright sun—that's what Burro Hills feels like in the summertime. I could feel it coming, the subtle shift in seasons, days stretching languidly, shadows falling longer and later.

We sat there in the stillness, watching the ripples across the water's surface. The Xanax was kicking in. Connor had given me several from his own huge prescription bottle, one I'd never seen before. I didn't ask about it, and he didn't elaborate. It didn't matter. Already it was easier to breathe, like time was slowing to a crawl.

I put my hand on his and squeezed his fingers. I didn't know if it was the drug or the deeply-rooted fatigue that made me feel so alive and frazzled and somber all at once. The smell of chlorine, the crickets, the peacefulness of it all…it was all starting to come together in a strangely lucid way.

I stood up and stripped down to my boxers, then plunged into the pool. It was warm from the sun, but cool enough to feel good on my skin. I surfaced and looked up at Connor. He grinned, then stripped down himself and dove in. We surfaced and floated on our backs, watching the sun melt across an orange Creamsicle sky.

"Everything in our human world is fake," I said.

"Yes," he said. "We do what we learn. We're all like robots, products of our environment. We think we're choosing things but we really aren't, you know? We're doing what we were inevitably programmed to do."

I looked up at the sky, into the beauty of the sunset. "How are things so beautiful and yet so ugly? People die every second, like, grisly, terrible deaths. People here live on the street in their own shit, starving, needle marks all across their arms, and yet the fucking sky looks like *that.*" I thought of Max then, what he would say. He'd bring up some fucked-up video he saw online, grainy footage of a man's leg severed off by a train, someone's broken body on the streets of a war zone. Things you never saw in the news. But they were real, with no added segments, no jaunty music or cut-ins. That was life.

The soft splashing of the pool and the drug made me feel like my muscles had evaporated, like I was floating through empty space.

A flock of birds flew over us in perfect formation, the sound of their wings beating silence into submission.

A dull, dreamy sleepiness was taking over me. Connor and I were drying off in the last touch of daylight, sharing a plastic recliner by the pool. "I'm sorry," I said to him, putting my lips to his collarbone. "I shouldn't have shut you out or pushed you away."

"It's okay," he said. He ran his fingers through my scalp the way I liked as birds tweeted their dusk-time songs. Cars rushed by across the way, close enough so we could hear their honking but far enough from the prying eyes of their drivers. It was peaceful here, with no one to judge us or try to make us feel like we had to be anything other than what we were.

"I've been thinking about it, and I think I want to tell

people about us," I said. "Maybe. I go back and forth. But I never want you to feel like I'm ashamed of you, because I'm not."

"I know you're not," he said.

"Because honestly…I love you. I love you so much, and I would never do anything to hurt you. I'd never let anyone hurt you either. I would kill for you."

I must've been higher than I thought because things were spilling out of my mouth like liquid. I didn't care if it sounded cheesy or emotional, or even if he didn't love me back. The freedom of being able to say those words and feel those things was like being able to fly.

"There's really nothing to be afraid of, Jack," Connor said.

That's when my phone chimed. I immediately checked, hoping that it was Jess, but it wasn't. It was a flurry of texts, all from Toby.

SOS.

Big problem.

Come to the garage.

Please.

And then, a few seconds later: *I need you.*

50

I thought about ignoring Toby's texts. I thought about calling him and telling him to fuck off, to never speak to me again. But the more I thought, the antsier I got. I had to confront him eventually. It might as well be now. And yet, I wondered about the SOS. Connor didn't even try to stop me. It was like he wanted to go. He walked fast, with purpose, holding my hand and pulling me along even though only I knew the way to get there.

We took the bus from the community pool a few stops to the garage, the old, abandoned auto repair shop that Toby's parents had once owned. The one that had killed them slowly over the course of long, hard-worked years. The one that had been meant for Toby someday, when he was old enough to work there and maybe own it himself.

Now it sat vacant, paint peeling off its dull concrete walls, the big MILLER AUTO REPAIR sign above the entrance vandalized and hanging all crooked.

Well, it was mostly vacant anyway. I hadn't been in there since before the death of Toby's parents. But I knew what his uncle and cousins used it for now. It was one of their meeting spots.

We were at the back entrance, near the office where his mom used to sit at the desktop and crunch numbers all day. The little metal door was covered in cobwebs now. Somewhere in the near distance a dog snarled, a big, mean one. A siren blared as a cop car raced up the street, lights flashing.

It occurred to me that we shouldn't be here. This was dangerous.

I knocked three times.

I heard shouting from inside, deep male voices arguing. "*Who the fuck is that?*" More shouting. Then the door swung open with a creak and there was Toby.

He looked terrible. His broken nose was covered in a huge bandage, but there were other bruises on his face, and deep purple marks along his wrists and arms that Connor couldn't possibly have caused. Like someone had been grabbing him roughly, violently.

As soon as he saw me, he smiled a little, this sad, relieved smile, like he was genuinely happy to see me. But then he noticed Connor, and his smile disappeared.

"Seriously? You brought *him*?"

"Nice to see you too, Toby," Connor said.

Toby just stood there, swaying back in forth in the doorway, as if unsure of what to do. He had this look in his eyes. Wild animal prey paralyzed. It was scaring the shit out of me.

"Can he leave?" Toby asked. He looked to me pleadingly. Like we were still friends. Like nothing had happened between us these past few weeks. Like he hadn't harassed me for days and called me a faggot. Like he hadn't tried to rape my best friend. "Jack. Please?"

I wanted to hit him as much as I wanted to help him. I shrugged and stared at my sneakers.

"No," Connor said. "I'm not leaving him alone here. Are you gonna tell us what's going on or what? Why you sent us all these messages?"

"*Us*?" Toby spat a wad into the wilting grass. "I sent them to Jack, not *you.* Jack, please. Make him leave." He lowered his voice. "We got a tip that the cops are on the way to our house. They're gonna raid it. The whole thing. Please, Jack. I just need you to talk to these guys and tell them that I didn't—"

"*Toby, who the fuck IS that?"* boomed a familiar voice. The angry male voices were arguing again. I backed away instinctively as D'Angelo's big, muscular frame appeared in the doorway.

"Oh," he said. "I remember you two punks. Why are they here, Toby? Why the fuck are they here? What were you thinking?" He slapped him upside the head, hard, and Toby just shrank back like a dog who'd been kicked. Shit. I'd never seen D'Angelo raise a hand to him before. Another police siren blared not so far off. D'Angelo cursed. "Get inside, both of you, before someone sees."

I wanted to run. My feet told me to run. Get the hell out of there, *now*. But strangely, Connor walked forward confidently, calmly, as if there was nothing to fear. I couldn't leave him. I followed him inside and the door slammed shut.

D'Angelo locked the door.

It was so dark in here. It smelled like sawdust and fumes and something burning. As my eyes adjusted, I spotted five or so guys I kind of recognized—big guys, including Toby's uncle, who was smoking a fat cigar, and Gabriel. They were seated in the center of the garage at a long, metal folding table. And they were all staring at us.

"Who the fuck is this? That you, Jack?" Toby's uncle asked sharply. He knew me. He saw me all the time at Bazingo. But the way he was looking at me now, it was like I was a cockroach he'd just stepped on. He pointed at Connor. "Who is *this*?"

"I didn't invite him!" Toby said quickly. "I just invited Jack. He knows us, the family. He knows the whole situation. He can explain everything."

I can? What did he want to me to say?

"Well you better start explaining now," D'Angelo growled. "First you bring a girl to the house. You *never* bring a girl to the house. Are you dumb or are you stupid?

Then she goes to the pigs, says something about you *sexually assaulting* her? Tells them shit about what she *saw* in our house? When they're already suspicious? And now they have probable cause to enter. What is wrong with you, Toby? Do you want your entire family to go to *prison*?"

Jess. Jess had called the cops on Toby. I felt for my phone in my pocket but didn't dare take it out. Not yet. Not with all these guys' hard, mean eyes on me. I had to get out of here and find her, help her. Do whatever I could. I tugged at Connor's sleeve. We had to go. Whatever trouble Toby was in now, there was nothing we could do. But Connor pulled away from me, stepped forward, and got right in Toby's face.

"So you admit it, then?" he said. "You did assault her. Wow. You're a bigger pussy than I thought."

"Connor," I tried. "Let's go. Please. This doesn't involve us."

Toby's hands clenched at his sides. "Oh, but I think it does, Jack," he said. He jabbed his finger into Connor's chest, but Connor didn't even flinch. "*You're* the reason all this started. If it wasn't for you, none of this would have ever happened!"

"We don't have time for this high school drama," Gabriel said. "Get them out of here, Ang."

But D'Angelo put a hand up, like he wanted to see what would happen next. His eyes were fixed on Toby and Connor. And they were hungry eyes.

"No, Toby, you're the reason your friend now thinks you're a worthless asshole."

"That kid is my *brother*!" he screamed, pointing at me. "The only worthless asshole here is you!"

"You treat all your brothers like that, Toby? At least when I fuck Jack, he likes it."

Toby shoved him. Connor shoved him back harder. Toby stepped back a few paces and put his hands up defensively. He was frightened, and not just of Connor I realized, whose own fists were balled, who was somewhere else entirely. D'Angelo was looming behind them, licking his lips, eyes wide and ravenous.

Shit, shit. I gingerly slipped my phone out of my pocket and dimmed the lights, sending my location to Connor's uncle along with a *Call 911* text while everyone else was watching the brewing fight. *Drug gang*, I added, just to be safe.

"It was him," Toby said to D'Angelo. He pointed at Connor. "He was the one who fucked over this family! He probably told that slut to call the cops. And I know for sure he ratted us out."

"Shut up, Toby!" I said. "You know that's bullshit."

D'Angelo's expression shifted. "That true, Toby?"

Toby nodded vigorously. He wiped the sweat pooling off his face.

D'Angelo moved towards Connor, but again, he didn't flinch. "You fuck over my family?"

Connor looked him in the eye. "Fuck your family."

It all happened so fast.

D'Angelo's punch knocked Connor to the ground. All of the breath left my body. Then he was on him, kicking him with his steel-toed boots. I tried to get in there, but a sharp pain shot through my shoulder as one of the big guys grabbed me and pulled my arms behind by back. They were surrounding him now, all the rest of them, some watching, some joining in, some yelling at D'Angelo to pull back, cut it out.

"Leave him alone! Hit me instead!" I shouted, uselessly, hopelessly, but of course no one was listening. D'Angelo was kicking and punching Connor like a rag doll as I struggled to get loose of the arms that held me back.

The police sirens were back, louder this time. There was banging on the door. "POLICE! OPEN UP!"

SMASH. SMASH. They were trying to bust the door open. *Hurry, hurry,* I thought.

I don't remember what happened with the other guys, with D'Angelo and Gabriel and the uncle, but a few of them must have tried to make a run for it through another exit. Toby was still going out at it, punching and kicking Connor like he was in a fever dream, screaming bloody murder, until I ran up and pushed him off him, feeling warm blood in my hands. I saw Connor's closed eyes and limp body and realized that I was screaming too.

Then the police were inside, shouting, guns at the ready, barking at all of us to get on our knees and put our hands behind our heads. Toby was shoved to the ground and handcuffed, and there was more pain as my knees hit the concrete. This wasn't real. This wasn't happening.

An ambulance was called. Arrests were made of those they could find. The cops took me outside, practically dragging me, and there was Alvaro, his face a tight mask of pain and rage. He said something to the cops that made them unhand me. Something about me being a minor and a bystander.

As they took away Toby, our eyes met for just a moment. I looked away. I said nothing. I felt nothing.

I was nothing.

The cops questioned me. I remember that. It was like they questioned me for hours, as I stood there shaking in the front yard outside of the Miller Auto Repair shop as the sun began to set. I kept repeating myself, repeating all that I could say: "I don't know. I just showed up. I'm seventeen. My friend said he needed help so I came. My other friend came with me. From school. I'm in high school. I don't know what happened here. I don't know these guys. I don't know."

They must have figured out I wasn't enough of a threat, or at least they had bigger fish to fry, because this one woman cop with nice eyes and a gentle voice and her partner offered to give me a ride to the hospital. I sat in the back of their squad car, the police scanner crackling with voices that I couldn't make any sense of, watching the dark blur of the trees giving way to street lamps and eventually the freeway. It was dark now. It had never been more serene, more beautiful, the houses and all of the lights and cars melting into one calm, steady stream.

The waiting room was a cold, florescent plastic. I sat in a plastic chair, listened to the beeps and buzzes and crying and loud complaining of all the plastic people. I had to move away from them. I sat by the window, watching the ambulances pull into the giant garages, one by one by one.

Someone brought me some water. The woman cop. I sipped it once, then set it aside. It tasted like chemicals. She sat next to me and asked me more questions, about my parents, where I lived, what I was studying in school. I don't know what I said. I didn't know how to form sentences, words. After a while, she left.

A nurse approached me at one point and asked me if I was sure I didn't want to see a doctor.

"I want to talk to Connor," I said, my voice breaking. The sound of it startled me. It was raw, throaty and barely there.

"Your friend? He's in the ICU," said the nurse. "His uncle is with him. You'll have to wait a while. I'm sorry, honey."

They were playing *Wheel of Fortune* on the waiting room TV screens. I wondered if Mom was watching it now. I closed my imagined that she was here with me, holding my hand.

After a while I felt someone else sit next to me, and then felt small, gentle hands holding my tightly closed fists. They loosened and welcomed the fingers. I turned and there was Jess. Her face was puffy from crying. She kissed my cheek and leaned her head on my shoulder.

"How did you know to come here?" I asked.

"It's…all over the news, Jack. I thought you'd be here."

The warmth of her body felt nice. I briefly wondered if maybe I was hallucinating her, but the thoughts faded back into nothingness.

"Oh, Jack," Jess said. She started to cry, leaving streaks of mascara across her face like tire marks on hot pavement. I wanted to tell her it would be alright, but I didn't know what was up or down, what it might mean or not mean. I rested my head on her shoulder and found it hard to open my eyes.

The smell of freshly mowed grass, the sound of birds, a silent, dead morning. His coffin being laid to rest into the earth, years of secrets and hidden pain buried with it, everyone stone-faced and stoic except for me. I was screaming silently inside, a hollow shell of myself. A lone flower was dropped into the grave, a white rose.

Someone touched me and I gasped like I was coming up for air. I was back in the hospital, the chemical atmosphere flooding my senses. Alvaro was kneeling down to my level.

"He's okay, Jack, just banged up." He cleared his throat. His voice was heavy, like he was trying to lift bricks with his tongue. "He got knocked out, and it took a while for him to wake up. They've got him on fluids and painkillers now. Might be some fractures." He cleared his throat again, forcefully, his tone turning solid and stoic, like steel. "I do want to know what the hell you two were doing with those drug lords in possibly the worst part of town. I want to know everything, but for now, you don't look so good. Do you want to see a doctor?"

I shook my head.

"I called your dad. It took him a while to answer, but he answered. He's on his way over."

"He is?"

He nodded. "He's worried about you. He's going to take you home."

I moved to stand up. "I want to see Connor."

"He's resting, Jack." He patted my shoulder and I sat back down. "Just relax. It's going to be okay."

When my dad arrived, he didn't look drunk or slovenly, just confused, like an actor who'd walked onto the set of the wrong movie. He'd managed to shave and put on a decent shirt. A nice one. A button-down.

And when he saw me, he walked over so fast and

pulled me into a hug. I was too shocked to respond, to hug him back.

I don't remember much about the drive home. I think I dozed off.

All I remember is Dad didn't ask me anything, didn't yell at me, didn't say a word, and for that I was grateful. And he played the radio softly, my favorite station, and hummed along softly as he merged back onto the freeway.

51

It was all over the news—local, even national.

One of the biggest drug busts the police had seen around here in recent years.

D'Angelo and Gabriel and the uncle and most of the men from the garage, all of their mug shots were displayed. The newscaster's voice was low and rumbling, telling us that these local drug ring leaders had finally been caught after "what police believe to be a brutal gang-related attack on a local teen." A reporter standing in front of Toby's crumbling house, all blonde hair and white teeth and an approved-for-TV face of concern, telling us about this unassuming house in an otherwise quiet neighborhood. Yellow caution tape surrounded the property. DEA officers were everywhere.

The police wanted to talk to me again the next day at the station. This time, Dad went with me. He asked me if I wanted a lawyer, but I said no. I didn't need one. I didn't do anything wrong. He didn't question me. He just sat in the waiting room, reading a newspaper while I ratted out the boy who'd called me his brother to the local sheriff and a detective.

I told them everything I knew about that night, about Toby, about his family and the bits and pieces that I knew of their drug business. Things I'd seen over the years, things I'd witnessed. I left out my own involvement, of course. But it felt good to just talk, to let it all out.

And as it turned out, all of my stories corroborated with Toby's. He'd ratted out his entire family to the cops, told them everything he knew. My testimony might actually help him.

I should've hated Toby. I had every reason to. I should've wanted him dead.

But I didn't.

I told Alvaro everything too, as quickly as I could, standing in the station parking lot while Dad went to pick up a six-pack at the corner store next door.

I thanked him for saving our lives, for giving me his number.

"Seriously, I owe you."

"Anytime, kid," he said.

"When can I see him? How is he?" Connor's phone had gotten smashed sometime during the fight. I'd called the hospital a few times and asked to speak to him, but both times they'd said he was sleeping.

"He's alright. You can go see him anytime, Jack," Alvaro said. "You don't need my permission."

52

I didn't think I would cry, but I did when I walked into his hospital room. I just broke down at the sight of him.

His face and arms were bruised, his hand was bandaged, one eye was swollen shut, and everything was covered in hospital white, a white of death and loss.

He reached out to me, and I collapsed into him, my body wracked with sobs, crying even though I wasn't the one who should be, feeling humiliated and relieved all at once.

"Hey," he said, pulling my face to his. "Jack, It's okay."

"I'm so sorry," I said between gasps for air. I felt exposed, stripped to the bone, like all my wounds were naked and raw in this cold and uncomfortable room. "I shouldn't have taken you there."

"Jack," Connor's voice broke through my thoughts. "It's not your fault. Just sit down and listen to me for a second."

I sat down on the side of his bed, but I couldn't look at him. "Seriously, look at me," he insisted. He touched my face and turned it towards him. "It's not that bad. I know it's grisly, but just look at it."

I felt like I was out of my body, looking at the scratches on his neck like something had clawed him, the deep purple bruise on his collarbone, his one open eye glittering green.

"You can't be afraid of this," he said, gripping my arms, shaking me a little. "You have to let go of the fear. You can't live like this. I told you. You're letting them win. Look." He grabbed my hand and put it on his chest, right over his heart.

"Do you feel that? It's still beating. I'm alive." I nodded. I laid my head down on his chest and closed my eyes, letting him run his fingers through my hair, letting him comfort me, even though he was the one with the beat-up face and body. I could've stayed like that forever. "I have to tell you something," he said. "About me."

I waited while he took a deep breath, his chest rising and falling beneath me.

"I have this…compulsion, for lack of a better word. I do things sometimes. Okay, a lot of the time. Really dangerous shit. I get into these situations where I could die, where everything could fall apart at any minute, and it's almost like, that's when I feel the most alive."

I didn't speak. I just listened.

"I almost just ended it all, a few years ago. I wanted to kill myself." I swallowed hard. I'd known about the cutting, the burns on his wrist, but I hadn't known he'd wanted to take it that far. "I knew that if I took a bunch of pills and didn't wake up, I wouldn't really care. But then I thought about birth. It was weird. I don't know why, of all the things I've seen, that came into my mind. When I was really little, I saw my baby cousin being born, and her eyes were shut tight. I asked my parents if they'd been sewn shut, like if God had done that. Maybe He didn't want her to see us, I don't know. But when she opened them, and they were so beautiful, like almonds, I felt this joy, this joy I can't explain. I don't know if I'll ever really feel that kind of raw joy again, though I try to come back to it through memories.

"Anyway, I was debating on how I'd do it—whether I'd slit my wrists or not—which might be easier since I was so good at it—from all the practicing, you could say. For years I felt like I'd been swallowed into some black hole, and I couldn't breathe or see, like that baby, and I think that's when I thought of the birth, how somehow, through the blindness and the darkness, she came out…and she opened her eyes, and everyone loved her. That's when I decided not to do it, I think," he said. "But in a way, I haven't stopped trying since then. I never really stopped trying. But I'm done now, okay? I'm done trying to kill myself."

"How do I know that?" I asked. I remembered the way he'd called out the Rudoy brothers in the auditorium, even though they could've done the same thing to him that they did to Riley. The way he'd punched Toby. The way he'd burst through the door and into that garage full of criminals, ready to fight anyone and everything, ready for everything to explode.

He brushed away the wetness on my face.

"I guess you don't," he said sadly. "I guess I need help. I need to go back to therapy or something. I hated therapy, but I promise will. I promised my uncle. I don't want to die. I want to live. I really want to live."

"Mr. Orellana?"

I sat up as we turned around to face the doctor, a kindly looking older man with wire-rimmed glasses. "How are you feeling?"

"Good," he said. "Some pain in my shoulder, but I'm feeling a lot better. The morphine drip doesn't hurt."

"Well that's good to hear," he said. "And you'll call the nurse if you need more, yes?" Then he nodded in my direction and offered me a friendly smile. "And uh, are you his brother?" I wondered for a moment if he'd seen my head on

Connor's chest, his fingers threaded through my hair, and a part of me wanted to hide. But I shook my head.

"No," I said. "I'm his boyfriend."

53

Dad let me take the next few days off of school. He even called Principal Oliver on my behalf, told them I'd been present for the incident at the garage and that I needed some time.

I wonder what Oliver thought of me, of my and Connor's involvement. But I guess he wasn't angry about it, because when Dad got off the phone with him he just shrugged and said, "You're good."

Jess agreed to bring me the homework and assignments that I'd missed. Not that I'd really be reading or doing them, but it was the thought that counted.

She showed up at my house at two p.m. on Monday with her backpack full of papers and this smile on her face that said everything was going to be okay. We retreated to my room.

It was a beautiful, blue sky day. The air was cooler, cleaner, and I had my window open to let in the breeze. I'd cleaned up before she came, put away dirty socks and clothes, wiped some spilled soda stains off my bedside table. I'd even done a load of laundry.

"Looks nice in here," said Jess, nodding her approval. She tossed her backpack on the floor and flopped down on my bed. I half-expected her to launch into her usual saga about what everyone was up to at school, the fights and the drama, but instead she got really serious.

"We do need to talk," she said.

"Yeah," I said.

"Will you at least roll me a joint first?"

"Really?"

"Yeah, really. You're not the only one who smokes, you know."

I laughed and got out my rolling papers and grinder and the little bag of weed I had left. I'd resolved to quit after I ran out of the last batch Toby had bought for me, but part of me knew that was bullshit.

I was probably always going to be a stoner.

Jess ran her fingers along the zigzag patterns on my bedspread. "Can you do me a huge favor and not say anything until I'm done?"

I mimed zipping my lips shut and nodded. She sighed and spoke to the zigzags.

"You hurt me, Jack. You really did. And I know you know that. But you have to understand, what you did at that party was unbelievably wrong. And selfish. And cruel. You violated my body, and you violated my trust. I don't really care if you were trying to work out your sexuality or whatever. That's not an excuse. I also don't care if you felt like Toby and Max were holding your feet to the fire. Or that you were drunk. Or that I was drunk."

I licked the glue strip on the rolling paper and nodded, waiting for her to continue. Her words hurt like hell, but they didn't kill me. I could hear this.

"And I don't need another apology. I know you're sorry. What you do going forward matters more than what you say, in this case. And…when Toby…when he got on top of me and tried to rape me, I thought back to that night, and you. And how maybe I could never really be friends with a guy again. Like every guy I thought I could trust was eventually going to hurt me and use me. And it was the worst fucking feeling in the world. I just broke down. And I couldn't tell my friends, not Skye or Anna or Lizzie or anyone. I was like, embarrassed. Which is weird, right? What did I have to be embarrassed about? I thought, maybe I'd led him on. Maybe it was my fault. But my mom wouldn't stop asking me what was wrong, why I wasn't sleeping, why I looked so miserable all the time, so I finally caved and told her. And you know what was amazing? She listened. She didn't tell me what to do. And she cared and was like, 'Jessica Michele Velez, this is absolutely *not* your fault.' And she asked me what *I* wanted to do. And I said I wanted to go to the police and report it, even if it meant people at school were going to call me a slut and a liar. And I did, even though I could tell the police didn't really take me seriously, and they probably just wanted to talk to me to get whatever info I had on what I'd seen in his house, which I gladly gave them. But I'm also glad I told people." She finally looked up from the zigzags. "Anyway, I've decided that I'm going to give you another chance. Even though you can be a clueless, self-centered asshole. And I don't want you to tell me you're going to be a good friend to me. I want to you show me, okay? No more bullshit."

I offered her the freshly rolled joint. She grinned as I placed it between her lips and lit her up. She inhaled deeply, like a pro. Didn't even cough.

"You can talk now," she said, blowing smoke out of the side of her mouth. "I'm done. And a little stoned."

"Already?"

We both laughed.

"Okay," I said. "No more bullshit. Agreed." I chewed at my thumbnail. "You should know though." *Just say it*, I thought. *Just tell her.*

"Jess, I'm in love with Connor."

"Oh, honey," she said. She reached over and touched my hand. "I know."

54

I went to visit Mom at the Castle Motel on a day that the sky was thick with storm clouds. The humidity clung to the air, leaving a sticky, sweaty residue on my skin.

Summer was coming up, which meant no school for a few months. Which meant I probably should take summer classes, or at least get a job of some kind if I had any hope of getting out of here, or—maybe, just maybe—going to college someday.

It was the same motel Mom had taken me to when I was little, when I thought she was rescuing me from my father by whisking me away to the magic castle.

There were leaks in the ceiling, prostitutes hanging around outside. Cockroaches skittered around the dirty tiles of the bathroom floor. It was definitely no castle, and nothing like I'd remembered it. But she seemed happy. Her face was bright and clean, and she was dressed in jeans and a t-shirt, her hair pulled back into a loose ponytail. She looked years younger.

I sat down with her on the bed with the broken box spring and took her hands in mine. "Mom," I said. "I miss you. You should come home."

She gave my hands a squeeze. "I can't do that, sweetie. You know, I'm going somewhere great. I'm going to go see the world, Jack. You have to understand that I need to go. And I can't take you with me, baby."

She really meant it. She really thought she was going to go on some grand adventure. Or at least, that's what she wanted me to believe.

I kissed both of her hands. "I love you, Mom. Promise you'll come visit sometime, yeah?"

She grinned that knowing grin of hers. "How about you come visit me when I make it rich and move to Vegas, huh?" she asked, pressing a handful of lotto tickets against my chest. I didn't ask where she'd scrounged together the money to buy them. It didn't really matter.

She said she wanted to see the bison in Wyoming, the Rocky Mountains, and the Statue of Liberty. She promised she would write me and text me photos of everything new along the way. And that she would visit me. I swallowed hard to stop myself from crying and hugged her goodbye, telling myself it was better this way, even though it hurt more than I thought it would.

A few days later, her brother drove down from L.A. to get her. Dad said she'd be staying with him for a while so he could get her some real help. He had the money and the means.

Dad was still drinking, but he was calmer now that

Mom was gone. Quieter. He didn't yell or come home blasted drunk anymore. He fed and walked Gunther and did the dishes and even the laundry. For a solid week, he went to work, came home, and watched TV before going to bed. One night we even watched *Pulp Fiction* together and laughed at all of the same parts. I cooked a few times, or at least I tried to. Not that Mom had ever done much cooking. Mostly we ordered pizza and Chinese and ate frozen dinners.

It was good. It was fine. I didn't explain anything about Connor and me or the night of the attack, and he didn't ask. Maybe, I thought, he didn't really want to know.

There were rumors at school that Jess had been the one to seduce Toby and then called the cops after he'd dumped her to get revenge. Others whispered that Toby was a serial rapist and a kingpin and was probably going to prison for at least twenty years.

The truth was, Toby was in deep shit—like, really deep shit—but not twenty years deep, exactly. He'd gotten a good public defender who'd convinced the court that he was just a minor, just a pawn in a much bigger chess game. My testimony had apparently helped him. And he'd willingly told the cops everything about his involvement in the family business, all of that distribution and trafficking he'd been linked to.

As for the attack on Connor that night in the garage, well, Connor didn't want to press charges. He just wanted the whole thing to be over with.

Toby was sentenced to juvie until he turned eighteen. Then it was the county men's prison for the next three to five years. But he could be paroled for good behavior, could get his sentence lessened. He could appeal. I read all about it online, in a bunch of forums and sites where people were absolutely obsessed with his family and the case.

I thought about visiting him, asking him why he'd done it all to me. I thought about being a witness at one of his trials or appeals.

But I decided that it was over. I was done. I stopped reading the forums and the articles.

I didn't owe him anything.

But I did start talking to Max again. He'd called me a bunch of times since the night of the attack to see how I was doing, to make sure I was okay. I was still kind of mad at him for all the shit he and Toby had pulled together, but I couldn't really fault him for it. I'd done some terrible things myself.

Connor's return to school wasn't a total disaster. He insisted on going back as soon as he was well enough to leave the hospital. I stayed over at his house the night before, and we stayed up all night and talked about it, like how things would be from now on. In the morning, Jess picked us up and drove us to school in her brand-new Toyota Corolla, courtesy of her hoity-toity mother.

It was 6:30 a.m., and dark bruises were blooming across Connor's cheek. His swollen eye was just starting to open. It hurt when he breathed. One of his fingers was broken and in a splint. But he was healing, and he was going back. We were doing this together, even though it made me so nervous I thought I'd throw up right in Jess's brand new car, which she couldn't stop raving about, blasting rap music as we pulled up to the school. There was a sizable crowd forming out front, waiting around for the first bell. My stomach dropped at the sight of them.

"We're gonna be okay," Connor said, and leaned in to kiss me for the first time in front of Jess. It didn't help the thumping in my chest.

Buses were pulling in, and kids were crowding around in their usual packs. Connor and I walked hand-in-hand into the fray. Some people stopped talking and started staring and whispering. Jess trailed behind us. She was there for moral support. She also had plans to formally introduce Connor to the Spot after school.

One girl tried to approach Connor and ask him a question, but her friend quickly reprimanded her. I spotted some asshole taking photos of us on their phone, probably sending out a video to everyone they knew. It was funny how Connor had come to Burro Hills High a kind of celebrity, and now he was even more of one.

A group of freshmen guys started yelling something at us, something that was anything but friendly.

"Just phase them out," Connor said in my ear, and I nodded. "Remember that they're young and ignorant."

"*We're* young and ignorant," I said, and he smirked. I took a deep breath, counted to infinity, and leaned in. Fireworks went off in my stomach. I kissed him, and it was no Girl Scout kiss either. It was a kiss for every time I'd been called a faggot, every time I'd feared for the worst, or pushed him away, or hurt myself for how I felt about him. It was a kiss for loss and heartache and hatred, for spilled blood in the garage and screams and silence. The voices around us faded to a dull, white noise. Nothing else mattered. The sun hit us full on, and with his lips against mine, I smiled.

To my surprise, some people started cheering. There was booing and a few homophobic slurs mixed into it all, but the roars of applause and whistles seemed to drown it all out. Just for that moment, we were the center of everything, orbiting the solar system of our school, until a security guard who'd been perched nearby swooped down and broke us up.

My whole body was tingling, radioactive and alive.

"That was amazing," Jess told us moments later, after the crowd has dispersed, hecklers and cheerleaders alike. I inhaled her familiar conditioner and perfume as she pulled me into a warm hug. "That was so fucking brave, Jack."

I shrugged. "I just made out with someone in front of the entire student body and administration. I'd call that more exhibitionist than brave."

"Fair point."

Whatever it was, our public make-out session didn't cause the uproar that I thought it would. I went to class that day with my stomach full of acid, anticipating the worst, but people were surprisingly friendly and nonchalant. The Rudoy brothers were still douchebags, of course, but they kept their distance even when they gave us the side-eye. Rumor had it they were on behavioral probation of some kind, and one more infraction would get them kicked off the football team for good. I gave them two weeks.

Jason Xiang even approached us at lunch and asked how long Connor and I had been dating. My face got so hot, and I started to stutter like a loser, which made Connor start cracking up. But Max saved me by interrupting with an invite to his house party next weekend.

Smooth. He had my vote for SGA president.

It was so bizarre, like living in a dream world, a stark punch to the gut of a not-so-bad reality. I started hating Burro Hills High a little less, even the ugly orange lockers.

There was just one person left I kind of wanted to tell.

55

In the yard, under the growing pepper tree he'd planted just years ago, Dad was kneeling in the dirt. He wore overalls and gardening gloves, clawing a rake through damp ground. I watched him from my bedroom window. During the night, a storm had finally broken through the humidity, and now the air felt cool and smelled clean from all the rain.

Gunther moaned and put a paw in my lap. He was curled up in bed with me as I took hits off my *Ren & Stimpy* bong for courage. I scratched his ear and he sighed deeply, resting his head on my chest. I pet his graying muzzle.

"I miss Mom too," I said into his ear.

She'd been leaving me voicemails. She kept promising postcards to come, handwritten letters. She kept saying that one day, maybe, she'd come home.

Home. What exactly was home for Mom? I thought of all of those fights, all of that anger and pain, all of those times she tore up the house, breaking everything in front of her, throwing more and more gasoline on the fires of our chaos.

All of those times, I'd thought it was just Dad. The angry, shouting monster. I'd thought that as long as he was around our family had no hope.

By the time I came outside to join him, Dad had made great progress on his little makeshift garden.

"Coffee?" I asked, holding up a warm mug for him, the one that had my kindergarten picture laminated on it.

When Dad looked up at me, something struck me about his face. There were the same wrinkles, the same baggy eyes, but there was brightness there, a softness that I hadn't seen in forever. He thanked me and patted the wet grass where I kneeled beside him. He showed me what he was planting.

I need to tell you something, I thought, as Dad told me all about the balloon flowers and crested iris he had bought at the hardware store. *There's something I want to tell you.* Fat pink worms wriggled in the mulch he'd put down, struggling to free themselves from their drowned homes. Dad sipped his coffee, cleared his throat, and put his hand on my back.

"This is nice," he said.

I nodded. Words were caught and tangled up in me. A thousand sentences ran through my head like ticker tape.

Then he surprised me. "You want to get a pair of rubber gloves on and help me? There's a couple in the garage."

We spent the next two hours making flowerbeds and planting seeds. Maybe I would tell him when we were done planting, when we'd gone inside and wiped the mud off our pants and shoes. Maybe I'd tell him later that night over a screening of *Boogie Nights,* which I'd recently discovered was one of our shared favorite movies. Maybe I'd tell him later that week, or that month, or when I invited Connor over and formally introduced him as someone other than my friend.

Maybe I never needed to tell him at all.

A light drizzle began, but we didn't stop to go inside. We worked with the earth until our hands were sweaty inside the rubber gloves, our arms sore from raking, our feet tired. We tilled the ground beneath us, and for one long expanse of time, the air between us was free of exhaust fumes.

RESOURCES

The Trevor Project
Chat at thetrevorproject.org
Call 1-866-488-7386

National Sexual Assault Telephone Hotline (RAINN)
Chat at rainn.org
Call 1-800-656-4673

National Suicide Prevention Lifeline
Chat at chat.suicidepreventionlifeline.org
Call 1-800-273-8255

ACKNOWLEDGMENTS

This book is nearly five years in the making, and it wouldn't exist in its current form without the help and guidance of some truly incredible people.

To my agent, Saritza Hernández, for being the one to give me and this book an enthusiastic "YES," and for fighting so hard and for so long to get it into print. I can't thank you enough. And to Cate Hart at Corvisiero Literary Agency, for reading and offering your insight on one of the earlier drafts.

To my editor, Jaime Levine, for the hours spent brainstorming with me over hummus and pita, and for rooting for this book from the very beginning. You understand these characters so well and helped me take this story to a level I never knew was possible. And to everyone else at Diversion Books who worked so hard on this book: Erin Mitchell, Sarah Masterson Hally, Kayla Park, Angela Man, and the IPS Sales Team.

To my mom, dad, and sister, Jessie: I wouldn't be where I am today without your never-ending love and support.

Thank you for always pushing me to follow my dreams and for always believing in me.

To my amazing beta readers: Tegan, Bianca, and Ajax. And to the wonderful writing communities at Agent Query Connect and Absolute Write. You know who you are! You rock.

To my inspiring, awesome, amazing Electric Eighteens debut support group: seriously, thank you! You're all so unbelievably talented, and I don't know what I would have done without you.

And of course, last but obviously not least, to you, the reader. Thank you for holding this book in your hands, in the format of your choice, and for giving me my reason to keep writing. This one's for you.

JULIA LYNN RUBIN is a graduate of The New School's MFA in Writing for Children & Young Adults program. Her short stories have appeared in publications such as the *North American Review, Riprap Literary Journal*, and *Sierra Nevada Review*. She lives in Brooklyn, where she is currently working on her next young adult novel.

Follow her on Twitter **@julialynnrubin**, and visit her online at **www.julialynnrubin.com**.

CPSIA information can be obtained
at www.ICGtesting.com
Printed in the USA
BVOW09s1125130318
510013BV00002B/4/P